SNOWBOUND SUMMER

(THE LOGAN SERIES BOOK 3)

SALLY CLEMENTS

LARGE PRINT

ONE

Houses talk.

In the middle of the night—when sounds of the day have silenced, the noises that a house makes can be heard. Floorboards creak and squeak. Pipes bang as though tapped with invisible hands. Windows rattle at a gust of wind.

Summer Costello lay in the bed that had been hers since childhood listening to the familiar sounds. Eight long years ago she'd left home. Tonight was the first night back in her childhood bed. Back in her childhood home. The experience was both familiar and strange. She'd never expected she would be back—especially under these circumstances.

A scratching, scraping sound.

She looked toward the window. A tendril hanging from the Boston vine that clung to the outside of the house whipped against the window. It needed pruning. Tomorrow, she'd get out the ladder and attend to it. That's if the weather improved; clambering up the ladder in a howling gale was totally out of the question.

At least the kitchen was well stocked. She hadn't wanted to risk bumping into anyone in the local stores, so had done a large shop in a supermarket outside town on her way from the airport. There seemed no point in buying a turkey and all the trimmings, surely there could be nothing more pathetic than cooking and eating a Christmas dinner alone, so she'd stocked up with Christmas booze, chocolates, good coffee, and everything she'd need to cook simple meals.

Ma would be appalled to discover Summer had spent Christmas here alone. If she told her parents the truth, they would have cancelled their much-anticipated vacation in Spain with her brother. Would have stayed at home or paid for Summer to join them. She'd always been their golden girl—they'd be so disappointed in her if they knew the truth.

A high, keening sound. Summer tilted her head to the side and listened.

Again. She crept out of bed and walked to the

window. Pressed her ear against the cold glass and strained to hear the faint sound through the noise of the storm. Again she heard it—a high, frightened yowling. Some poor animal was out there.

Quickly she dressed in warm clothes and pulled on snow boots. She stuck her arms through the parka and padded downstairs.

When she jerked open the front door a frigid gust of air whipped long strands of hair against her face. From inside, she'd thought it was raining, but the ever-growing pile of small ice bullets pushing against the front door proved her wrong. *Hail.* She sniffed. The scent of snow was in the air.

The Costello family home was a few miles outside town and anytime it snowed the road became quickly impassable. Its aspect, halfway up the mountain leading out of Brookbridge, provided breathtaking views, but the flipside made navigating the narrow roads difficult in the snow unless you had a vehicle made for it.

The Ford Fiesta Summer hired at the airport didn't qualify.

The noise cut through the tempest again.

"Where are you?" She grabbed a flashlight from the hall table, stepped out and pulled the door closed.

The cold wind bit through her clothing. With jerky movements, she zipped the parka to the top, and pulled the fur-trimmed hood over her head. She played the beam of the flashlight out into the darkness, then back against the shelter of the house's walls, searching for the animal.

She'd dipped her chin down, but cold beads of hail struck Summer's face again and again stinging her forehead and cheeks as she circled the house. "Where the hell are you?" she muttered under her breath.

The cry again.

Summer's head jerked to the right, following the noise, finally homing in on the animal's location. The door to the woodshed was closed, but upon further examination, her flashlight revealed a hole at the bottom—a hole big enough...

She shot the bolt and stepped inside.

"It's okay." Her gaze tracked the beam to the wood stacked neatly at the back of the shed. To the piles of larger rings, yet to be cut, that littered the dirty cobbled floor. She played the light to the left. A pair of glowing eyes reflected in the darkness.

A dog.

Its breed was indeterminate in the darkness, but it was a large breed. Not skinny like a Lurcher, or powerfully built like a Doberman or Rottweiler, the dog was more like a wolf. Perhaps an Alsatian.

It lay on its side, its chest rising and falling rapidly. Its back leg was at an unnatural angle, and the light picked out a glistening black spot at the top of the leg.

"It's okay." She crouched to make herself appear less threatening and took a step forward.

The dog bared its teeth, and a deep growl issued from its throat.

———

IT WAS warm and snug in Nick Logan's hermetically-sealed apartment. He drained his coffee cup, stacked it in the dishwasher, and groaned at the sight outside the window. As usual, the weather forecasters had got it wrong. They'd foreseen the storm, but hadn't said anything about snow.

And snow there was. Inches of it.

The creak and snap of the metal letterbox, and then a flurry of mail hit the mat inside the door. Nick walked over and picked it up. Junk mail, junk mail, bill, junk mail, bill, postcard. He tossed all the items except the postcard onto the hall table.

A large black bull. With a grin, Nick flipped the card over.

Are you sure you won't change your mind? They're here and driving me crazy!

A scrawled D concluded the note from his best friend, Declan Costello. He'd been vaguely tempted by the offer of flying out to spend Christmas in Declan's new pad in Andalucía—who wouldn't be? After working all through the holiday last year, it was his partner in the practice's turn to be on call this year, so he had a week off—starting tomorrow. But the thought of playing happy families with Declan's parents for the week had cemented Nick's decision to defer it.

Two weeks in July. That's when he'd go. Declan had been in Spain for four months, and his job contract was for a year—there was plenty of time to take Declan up on his offer.

Nick grabbed the Land Rover keys off the table, picked up his coat, and left the house.

Traffic was light in Brookbridge, partly because it was early, but also because of the snow. The roads were covered; the council hadn't salted them yesterday, so conditions were treacherous. He pulled up outside Brookbridge Veterinary and parked.

The building was in darkness. As usual, he was the first one in. The practice didn't open for an hour, he'd have time to go through the paperwork and prepare for the day. He and his partner Sean were the principal vets in the practice and they employed another two vets and three veterinary nurses. Evie the receptionist rounded out the team.

Nick put on the coffee machine—they always

complained about the strength of his coffee, but drank it anyway—and walked to Evie's desk to scan the appointment book. Two operations—easy ones, a cat to be spayed and a dog to be neutered. Various smaller procedures.

He rotated the appointment book back into place and straightened.

The phone rang.

He glanced up at the clock. No-one would be expecting the office to be manned at this time in the morning—he should let the answering machine get it—but something made Nick snatch up the receiver. "Brookbridge Veterinary."

"Oh, thank goodness you answered," a flustered female voice said. "I really need your help."

"We're not actually open for another hour—"

"I understand, but I really need your help. I've been out all night with an injured dog—I can't get him inside, and he's so cold."

"What happened?" Nick picked up a pen and ripped a page off Evie's notebook. "Are we his vet?" Her voice sounded vaguely familiar, but he couldn't place her.

"I don't know who his vet is. I doubt he even has one. He's not my dog." She spoke quickly. "Look, I just didn't know who to call. I haven't lived here in years. He must be a stray, or have been dumped. His ribs are sticking out, and he has a frayed rope around his neck—maybe he was tied up and escaped or something. I didn't want to call the ISPCA... His leg is hurt and he can't walk..."

"Okay." Every animal, no matter the circumstances, deserved a chance. Nick made a snap decision. "I'll come out. What's your address?"

"It's sort of complicated."

He jotted notes as she explained the route out of town, mentally cataloguing all the houses. A lifetime in Brookbridge meant he knew practically everyone and had visited most of the houses in the immediate area for one reason or another.

"So you turn left, drive two miles, and the house is on the left..."

He'd stopped writing a few minutes ago. Had sat in Evie's chair and marveled at the fact that he'd somehow not recognized her voice instantly.

"Hello, Summer."

———

SUMMER BLINKED. "WHO IS THIS?"

The man on the other end of the phone cleared his throat. "Ah, this is Nick Logan. Declan's friend."

Nick Logan. She closed her eyes tight. Of course. Declan had said something about Nick training to become a vet, but she'd forgotten. She'd presumed he would have left the small Irish town when he qualified, that he would have struck out for a new town, or another country—not only would there be more opportunities for a vet in other places, but somewhere else would also be more exciting, more interesting. Before she'd even left school, she was planning to study overseas and exploit all the opportunities the big, wide world had to offer.

A brief memory of her younger brother's best friend flashed into her mind's eye. Nick Logan, seventeen, dressed in board shorts and lounging around in this very house's back garden, one hot, long ago summer. At twenty, he'd been here at this very house at her sendoff party.

"Nick. Wow, I haven't seen you in years."

"Three," he said quickly. "Declan and I came over to London for the opening of *Summer's Kitchen*."

Her pride and joy. The culmination of all her dreams. That night, her future stretched ahead full of wonderful possibilities. Michael had asked to move in with her that night, and with her friends and family around her it had been the best evening of her life.

She'd forgotten that Nick had also attended.

"Time flies." *Dreams die.* "So you're the vet now." She mentally face palmed at the obviousness of her words. *Duh, yes*...but she just kept talking, making it worse. "I mean, obviously you're the vet, um..."

She rubbed the back of her neck. She'd been determined not to meet anyone she knew in Brookbridge. Not to even confess that she'd spent Christmas in her parents' home alone until she felt strong enough to fasten the mask she always wore back in place. Nick must be wondering about her being in Ireland—he must know her parents were in Spain—she should say something.

He beat her to it. "I want you to explain this dog's injuries to me in as much detail as you can." His voice was impersonal and matter-of-fact. "Your road is always terrible in the snow, but I have a Land Rover, so I'll make it. I want to be ready for anything."

He'd cut through her waffle like a chef with a Sabatier.

Summer took a deep breath, and gathered her thoughts. "I think his back leg is broken, I can't get close enough to check, but it's at an odd angle, and there's a big cut with blood at the top of his leg. He's pretty wild. When I approached him last night he bared his teeth and growled at me. He's obviously frightened. I gave him a steak and he devoured it. After that, he stopped growling, but he wouldn't let me nearer. You should bring a tranquillizer." The dog was obviously frightened and traumatized. It was more than likely that the only option would be to put him down—an aggressive dog didn't have many options.

Any of the farms nearby would have shot the dog on sight.

"He may be beyond saving," she said. "But I can't just leave him out there. I have to give him a chance. Um..." Summer hesitated for a moment, then decided she had no option but to make the request. "I hate to ask, but could you bring some dog food with you?"

"Of course," Nick said. "Do you want me to bring you anything else? This weather is setting in—firelighters, milk, bread?"

She'd loaded up with most things but... "Firelighters and matches would be good. And I guess extra bread could be useful. I'm fairly well stocked, apart from those."

"Okay. I need to brief my colleagues here, so it'll be an hour or so before I make it out there." Brief, to the point, and efficient.

"That sounds great. Thanks, Nick."

She hung up. It had been one hell of a night. The dog had been unable to make it across the floor to where she crouched, but she had no doubt if he could, he would have attacked her. Maybe she was crazy even trying to save this dog.

TWO

Summer Costello.

Nick leaned back in Evie's leather swivel chair and closed his eyes. He hadn't seen her for three years but the mental image that popped into his mind was vivid. Average height, around five foot six, but that was the only thing average about her. She'd won every prize there was at school, and as well as excelling academically she had been captain of the hockey team and head girl. She'd been popular and confident, girls wanted to be her, and boys wanted to be her boyfriend.

The last time he'd really had a chance to speak to her was before she left to go to London. At twenty-two, Summer had worn her auburn-verging-on-red hair long, framing her face in unruly waves.

Her eyes were a vivid shade of blue he'd never seen on anyone else—her brother's were brown. Crushing on Summer's friends had been a popular pastime of his and Declan's, but Summer was always out of bounds. And for her part, Summer had never reciprocated his interest.

In fact, the very opposite.

Three years ago, the crazy dream of one day being with her had died forever.

Nick stood up and walked into the surgery to pack supplies he would need to treat the dog. Ideally, after sedation he would bring it back to the practice for surgery, but there was always the possibility that would prove impossible so he also packed the chemicals needed to put the dog to sleep.

A tinkling sound alerted him to the fact that someone had entered the building. In the reception area, Evie was hanging up her coat. Her hair was covered in a fine dusting of snow. She pulled a pair of slippers out of her voluminous handbag and toed off her boots, leaving them under the coat stand. "Good morning." She gave him a big grin. "Hell of a day out there, huh?" She brushed the snowflakes from her hair, slipped her feet into the slippers and rounded the desk to flick on her computer.

"Sure is. I guess by the look of you it's snowing again." He opened the door and stared across the car park. His Land Rover had turned white since he'd arrived three quarters of an hour ago.

"They're saying on the radio that it's going to get worse," she said. "They were giving that don't-travel-unless-you-have-to warning."

It was the worst possible time to drive into the mountains.

The bell above the door tinkled again and both the other vets dashed in.

"I had a call this morning," Nick explained as they shed their coats. "A woman has found an injured dog. I have to drive out there."

"Where?" asked Alison Cavanagh, one of the vets.

Everyone knew Summer and Declan's parents, and that they had left for Spain a week ago. If Declan had known Summer was in the house he would have told Nick, so he had to presume she was there without anyone's knowledge. He hadn't asked if she was alone—hadn't needed to, at Christmas everyone wanted to be with family, so her boyfriend must be there.

Still, something kept him from revealing her presence in Brookbridge. "The Land Rover is probably the only vehicle that will make it up the mountain in these conditions."

Alison frowned. "The weather is getting worse,

driving into the mountains…" She shook her head. "You shouldn't even try it."

"I have to. There's an animal in pain, I can't just leave it to die. You know me, Ali, I'll be careful. I have my phone and a blanket in my car. The Land Rover can handle any conditions, I'll be fine."

"Well, keep in contact," Alison said. "Check in the moment you arrive. If this weather gets worse you could be marooned."

"That's a chance I'll have to take."

Once upon a time, being marooned with Summer Costello would have been on his to-do list, but being marooned with her and her boar of a boyfriend would be pure torture. "The sooner I get out there the better."

———

SUMMER WAS on the point of phoning Nick again—it had been an hour and a half since she'd made the early morning call—when the distinctive sound of an engine cut through the silence.

"He's here," she said to the unresponsive dog. "Help is here."

In the past hour the dog had barely raised his head from the cold cobbled floor of the woodshed—even when she spoke to him—and the fight had gone out of his eyes. She'd gotten close enough to drape an old blanket over him in a vague hope of keeping him warm. The growl that issued from his throat was a faint and pathetic noise. He looked like he was staring death in the face and welcoming it.

"Hold on—just hold on a little longer." She left the woodshed and walked around the house to the front door.

A tall figure was climbing out of the Land Rover. The last time she'd seen him Nick Logan had been tall and skinny. Like her brother, he'd shot up in his late teens. This Nick Logan was different. He'd grown into his frame, and while he was still lean, he'd developed muscle. He'd always been a good-looking boy, but now, as a grown man, he was devastating.

"Hi, Summer." He slammed the door of the Land Rover and walked to her. "Good to see you." He enveloped her in a warm hug—which should have been no surprise—the Logans were notorious huggers. He'd hugged her when she left for London eight years ago.

She was pretty sure she hadn't felt anything back then, but being enveloped in Nick Logan's warm arms, breathing in his scent, sent a ripple of awareness through her now. So she stepped back as soon as was politely possible. "Hi, Nick." Her face felt hot. *Am I blushing?* She swallowed. "Thank you so much for coming out."

He and Declan had been friends forever—he must know she wasn't expected to be here.

To her relief he didn't question her. Instead, he grabbed a black doctor's bag from the back of the Land Rover. "Where's the patient?"

"He's different this morning." They trudged through the snow to the woodshed. The snow was still falling, dusting Nick's dark hair with snowflakes. "It's as though the fight has left him." Nick strode along next to her, not touching, but a tangle of awareness spread at his proximity.

She pulled open the door to the woodshed, pointing at the hole. "He must have crawled through here somehow." For the first time, she noticed a trace of blood on the broken wood.

The dog didn't look up as they approached. His eyes were closed.

"He was awake when I left." Her gaze focused on the dog's chest; relief flooded her seeing it rising and falling slowly.

"Ah, poor fella." Nick walked straight to the animal's side and placed his bag on the ground. He crouched. "How are you doing, fella?"

The dog's eyes flickered open, but he made no noise, probably too exhausted.

Nick reached out a hand and let the dog sniff him. "Okay, I'm not going to hurt you."

He continued talking in a low, comforting tone

that made the tension leave Summer's body. The dog, too, seemed to relax, mesmerized by the sound Nick's voice. Her breath caught as Nick stroked the dog's head. She wouldn't have had the courage.

Slowly, still murmuring, Nick lifted the blanket and ran his hands over the dog's flanks. He examined the cut on the back leg carefully. "He's in bad shape." He stood up and took a step back to where she stood. "You got him to eat something?"

"Yes, he had the steak I was going to have for dinner tonight."

Nick nodded. "That fits. He's badly malnourished and dehydrated. I don't think he'd survive the trip back to the surgery."

Summer felt a pain in her heart as though someone had wrapped their hands around it and squeezed. "You mean you have to put him down?" Her gaze flicked to the dog who opened his eyes and stared at them.

"No. But I can't treat him here, the conditions are filthy and there isn't enough light. I'll need the help of your boyfriend to carry him inside."

My boyfriend. "Michael isn't here." She couldn't bring herself to reveal the truth, that her three-year relationship had ended four months ago, and she hadn't seen him since. She crossed her arms. "I can help you get him inside."

NICK LOOKED out at the falling snow. Emotions mixed within him at her pronouncement. Curiosity, that her all-too-perfect investment advisor boyfriend wasn't here, and relief that he wouldn't have to deal with the city slicker sliding around in the snow in his shiny, black leather shoes. Michael was the sort of man who probably didn't even own a pair of jeans—he doubtless wore a suit five days of the week, and dressed in designer gear every weekend.

From the sarcastic snippets Declan had furnished over the years Nick had built up a fairly clear picture of the man Summer had chosen. Haircuts once a week, manicures every fortnight, and regular manscaping appointments at his salon.

The last time Declan had visited them in London, Michael offered to treat him to a back, sac and crack wax. When Declan returned to Brookbridge, they'd laughed their asses off in the pub at that.

Not having him here was a relief.

He looked down. The dog was young, maybe a couple of years old. She'd described him on the phone as an Alsatian, but he wasn't a pure bred—if Nick had to guess he'd say the dog was possibly half Labrador or collie as well. His size was intimidating, and the rope around his neck indicated he'd been tied up—probably used as a guard dog by someone with something to hide. He knew too well how the lives of many of these dogs went. They were permanently chained outside, infrequently fed, and encouraged to snarl and bark at strangers.

Even if he survived the significant health challenges that faced him, he might never be rehabilitated enough to become a family pet.

The dog's eyes flickered open; the expression in them made up Nick's mind for him. He looked like hell, looked as though he'd been living in hell, but he deserved a chance.

"I'm going to sedate him—it will take a few moments before he's out and then we can get him inside." He crouched at the dog's side again, took a syringe from his bag and carefully filled it. "Okay, fella, you will feel better soon." He located a vein in the dog's foot and injected him.

Then he stood up, brushed damp sawdust from his knees and turned to Summer.

Driving up here, he'd hoped that the years might have dimmed her beauty. That he might have grown out of the oversized crush that had tormented him through his teens and early twenties. Unfortunately, she was prettier than ever. Sure, there were a few more lines on her face—but they just added character.

It was a shame she was such a bitch.

While she stared at the dog, he looked closer. She wasn't wearing makeup, and didn't even seem to have brushed her hair, which was unusual for Summer—she'd always put great stock in looking good. There were dark circles under her eyes, and she seemed to have lost weight since the last time he'd seen her.

"Let's go inside. We need to prepare the kitchen."

"Okay." She cast a last look at the dog. "I hope he makes it."

"We should give him a name."

She smiled. "I think you've already done that—I reckon his name is Fella."

She talked away as they walked to the house. Summer had always been blessed with the ability to talk to anyone, anytime, and make them feel special. She excelled at charm—when it suited her. "I'd forgotten that you were training to become a vet," she confessed. "When I lived here the veterinary practice was around the back of Main Street—the vet was Patrick Jackson I think."

"He retired. My partner and I took over the business."

Her eyes widened slightly at the news, but she didn't comment. She pushed open the back door into the kitchen.

The warmth made his cold hands tingle. "You lit the wood-burning stove?"

"I thought that would be sensible. The heating is on, but if the power goes out..."

"Good." He walked to the heavy pine table, and started to clear it. "Have you an old oilcloth or something we can cover this with? There's likely to be blood."

Her face went pale, but she straightened her shoulders. "I'll get it. What else do you need?"

Nick thought for a moment. "A bowl for hot water. An old cardboard box and a couple of blankets."

"And a bowl for some water for Fella to drink?"

"Not right now—I've brought a drip to rehydrate him and he won't be taking anything by mouth for a while, but later, yes we'll need one for water and one for food."

She hurried from the room, and he shoved the table closer to the range.

THREE

Worry that had been a constant companion since she'd found Fella eased as Summer pulled open drawers in the storeroom off the kitchen where her mother kept all manner of odd things. When items were worn, they made the journey from the house to this room, and when they were completely beyond use, they were put out into the garage. Both her parents were borderline hoarders—letting go of stuff was difficult for them. When the garage got too full, they hired a skip and had a clear out. The garage was big enough that that event only happened every five years or so.

A gold colored trophy lay on top of sheaves of paper in the first drawer. She picked it out, and tested its weight in her hands. When she was twelve, the trophy she'd won at school for being the fastest sprinter had seemed a lot heavier. The papers underneath looked familiar too. She leafed through them. First in the regional spelling bee. First in debating. A couple of rosettes from the brief few years she'd taken up horse riding.

She shoved them back in the drawer, closed it, and opened another. *This is more like it.*

A carefully folded piece of worn oilcloth was shoved into the drawer, along with a bolt of material, an offcut from her mother's homemade curtains. She pulled out the oilcloth and opened it out to see if it would be big enough.

Satisfied, she folded it again, and shoved it under her arm. *Now, what else?* He'd said a cardboard box and a couple of blankets, presumably to make a basket for Fella. She glanced around. She could do better than that. A huge plastic dog basket was stacked up against the side of the room—something that should by now have been relegated to the garage—their old dog, Seb, had been dead for at least ten years. It was stacked with empty plastic ten-liter water bottles.

She moved the bottles to the floor, and struggled to ease the basket from behind a couple of old, broken down chairs, and tossed the oilcloth into it.

She would have to check upstairs for the blankets.

"How are you getting on in there?" Nick stuck his head in through the door.

"I've found these."

"Great." He took the basket and oilcloth. Their hands brushed, and a tingle raced up her arm. He stared into her eyes, and awareness of him spread like honey on hot toast.

Summer swallowed. "I'll just grab a couple of blankets."

"That can wait. The snow is getting heavier. We need to move Fella now."

The prospect of carrying an unconscious dog seemed impossible.

"I'll need an old board and a wheelbarrow." Nick smiled. "I guess we should check the garage."

Of course. He knew her parents as well as she did—when he hadn't been in his own house, he'd been in hers. He walked to the keys hanging on hooks at the side of the cooker, and instantly selected the right one. "Come on."

She followed him to the garage, where they found an old board—that had formed the side wall of the house her father had made for chickens years ago—laid it out on the wheelbarrow, and started back across the yard to the woodshed. "We'll move him, and then I'll bring in my stuff from the Land Rover."

———

EVEN THOUGH FELLA WAS EMACIATED, he was still a big dog, and it took a lot of effort to pick him up and place him on the makeshift stretcher. But they made it. She placed a hand on Fella's neck as he pushed the barrow to the back door, only letting go to open the door for him. She was getting attached. Maybe he shouldn't have suggested they give him a name—if he didn't make it, she'd be devastated. He'd seen this reaction before. People who saved animals and brought them to the vets always thought that the hard part was over, now the animal would receive medical attention and be saved. Unfortunately, sometimes there was nothing they could do.

He gritted his teeth, and pushed down the negative thoughts. He'd try everything to save this dog. Already, he was living on borrowed time—Fella had been starved almost to death, somehow escaped from whoever had tied the rope around his neck, and Nick suspected Fella had been hit by a car at some stage last night.

He deserved a break. A break Nick would do his best to deliver. "Okay, I'll take his shoulders, and you lift his back," he advised. They'd done it once, they could do it again.

She moved into position, and slipped one hand under the dog.

"Lift."

Together, they got Fella onto the kitchen table.

"Stay there with him. I'll be back in a moment." He pushed the wheelbarrow out into the yard, and tramped through the snow to the Land Rover.

When he came back, she was standing in exactly the same position as when he left. One hand on Fella's neck. There was a trace of sadness in her expression, and for a moment he feared the worst. "How is he?"

She turned, and an unsteady smile wavered at the corners of her mouth. "He's still alive." She looked at the things he was carrying. "Can I help?"

"I can manage. I brought a bag to rehydrate, but I forgot to bring a stand." He'd been in such a hurry it was inevitable that he'd forget something.

"Maybe...how about the coat stand from the hall? It has hooks on it."

"Yes, that'll work."

She dashed out into the hall and came back carrying the iron coat stand that Declan had bought his parents as a Christmas present years ago.

"Set it up over there." Nick pointed to the spot where he needed it. Then he went to the sink, and started to scrub.

She filled a bowl with hot water as he dried his

hands and put on latex gloves. The first thing he would do was insert a line for the drip, and then he would examine that leg.

"You might want to leave for a while." Not everyone was able to watch a dog being operated on, and the last thing he needed was her fainting.

"Don't you need me to help?" She stood her ground. "I'm not going to faint, if that's what you're frightened of." She looked offended that he'd even think it. "I've done my fair share of dissecting."

"Yes, but those animals and birds are dead, aren't they?" He grinned. She had spent nine months in the top Cordon Bleu school in London—he had no doubt she could reduce a cow to steaks without batting an eye, but dealing with living creatures was different.

"You need me to help." There was stubborn determination in her voice. "I'm up to it. What do you need?"

I need to stop being so bloody impressed by you.

"Attach the bag onto the coat stand hook while I insert the line." She picked it up, and did as he asked. Nick breathed in deep, and focused his attention back to his patient.

She stood at his side as he inserted the line, shaved around the cut with the razor he always carried in his surgery grab bag, cleaned the wound, and put Fella's dislocated leg back into the correct position. To his relief, the bone wasn't broken, but it would be badly bruised—Fella wouldn't be going anywhere for a while. He sewed up the deep gash in the animal's flesh, and disinfected it. "We should get him into the basket while he's out," he said. "We don't want him trying to climb off the table when he revives."

While he was stitching Fella, she'd found blankets and set the basket near the wood burning stove. Now, she helped him maneuver the large dog into the basket, which he more or less filled.

"How long before he wakes up?"

"It could be a while," Nick said. "The anesthetic is powerful, and he's exhausted, once he comes around, he'll be groggy and fall asleep again quite quickly."

Summer poured the pink-tinged water out of the bowl and washed it. Threw away the pieces of lint and other detritus that littered the table, wiped down the oilcloth, and took it off the table.

She folded it again and again, until it was a small parcel. "In that case, how about a cup of tea?"

"Sure. I need to make a call though first." Nick walked to the coat he'd thrown on a chair, put it on, and retrieved his cell phone. "I'll check conditions while I'm at it. Excuse me for a moment."

Fat flakes of snow drifted in the air, too light and unsubstantial to do anything more than float.

When he'd been a kid this had been the sort of snow he'd liked best. The type that stuck to your clothes and hair, converting you to a walking, talking snowman.

Today, his feelings were very different. Above, a swirling vortex of snowflakes filled the sky. The tempest of the previous night had blown itself out, but the snow just kept coming. He looked down. The path he'd tracked from the Land Rover earlier had practically filled in, his footsteps now just faint indentations in the tight packed snow. His speed increased until he reached the car, jerked open the door and climbed inside. He punched in the practice's number.

"Evie. It's Nick."

"How's the patient?" Just like the rest of the people in his employ, Evie was hardwired to think of the patient first.

"Well, I've stitched up his leg, and he's in recovery. I had to put in a line—he's dehydrated." He couldn't even see out of the windshield, cocooned in a bright, white soundless world. "There's no way I can transport him today, he's too weak. I'll have to stay the night here."

"Where is it you are exactly?" There was curiosity in her tone.

"I'm at Declan Costello's parents' house." He

crossed his fingers. "They have someone housesitting while they're in Spain."

"Oh, okay. I hope you have plenty of food in. This doesn't look as though it's going away any time soon."

She was right. "I'll call you tomorrow." He flicked off the phone and sat for a moment in the cold. *Stuck alone overnight with Summer Costello. Definitely not a good idea.*

———

SUMMER WATCHED Nick's tall figure stride out toward the car. It was hard to reconcile the confident capable man with the quiet teenager she remembered. Since the moment he'd arrived, he'd effortlessly taken charge, telling her exactly what he needed to do the operation on Fella.

He knew exactly what he was doing, and his calm focused approach to the task at hand had been extremely impressive. She'd caught herself just staring at him on more than one occasion as he cleaned the dog's wound and expertly sewed it up. Obvious care had overlaid all of his actions, and Fella couldn't have been in better hands.

Across the yard Nick climbed into the car and brought his cell phone to his ear.

Who is he calling? Probably a girlfriend. Maybe even a wife. She hadn't noticed a ring, but it was highly likely that with his job he didn't wear one. Her forehead wrinkled as she tried to remember what Declan had told her about his best friend in recent times. She couldn't remember talk of a wedding—a Logan wedding was always unforgettable, she was sure if Nick had married she would have heard all about it.

With a puff of frustration she turned away from the window to flick on the kettle. The state of Nick Logan's love life was none of her concern.

Summer wiped down the kitchen table and placed two mugs, a jug of milk and the sugar bowl on it. Her rumbling stomach reminded her she hadn't eaten all day. It was lunchtime now so she opened a can of soup and set it on the stove to heat.

By the time Nick pushed the door open a few minutes later, she'd transferred the hot soup into bowls and placed a couple of pieces of toast on plates.

He shed his coat in the doorway and brushed off the flakes of snow outside the back door then slammed the door behind him. He was carrying a couple of bags, which he placed on the kitchen counter. "You told me he ate your steak so I brought you another. I brought one for me as well—the cooking is up to you."

He pulled out a wrapped packet. "The

anesthetic may make him feel sick and apart from that steak Fella may not have eaten for a while. It's likely his digestive system is in uproar so we should start off with something basic to eat rather than the dog food I brought." He held up the package. "Chicken. If we just boil this he should be able to handle it."

"Sure. Leave it there and I'll cook it after we eat." She found a couple of linen napkins, slid them into napkin rings, and placed them next to the bowls. Waved at the table. "Come eat, before it gets cold."

He sat. "You're the only family I know who uses these." He slipped the napkin from the ring and turned it around in his big hands.

"I bought them when I was seventeen. And these table mats too. I'd been watching all these cooking shows—the Galloping Gourmet was my favorite and at the end of every show he invited someone from the audience to sit down and taste what he'd cooked. It was always presented beautifully."

"I remember you were always into presentation." There was the hint of a double meaning in the way he said the words.

"Presentation matters."

"Not as much as you might think." He shook out the napkin and placed it over his knees. He picked up the spoon. "Substance is more important. You can make a table look as pretty as you like, but if the food doesn't taste good, no amount of prettying it up will make a jot of difference."

He dipped a spoon into the soup and tasted it. "Now this is a win—in both aspects."

"Well, it's canned." It was pretty difficult not to extrapolate Nick's philosophy on food into the area of humans. Michael had always been perfectly presented—the male equivalent of a table set with fine china, sparkling silverware, placemats, napkins and crystal glasses. But at the end of the day he left a bad taste in her mouth.

"So, you made your phone call."

"Yes—I let Evie know where I am."

Evie. So he has a girlfriend.

"I'll have to stay the night. Fella isn't well enough to travel, and a lot of snow has fallen since I arrived—the trip into town would be treacherous. With any luck, the council will send out a team to salt the road tomorrow."

It was snowing so hard that it was as if a white curtain was fluttering in the air. An ever-changing pattern so bright it was difficult to look at.

"If we aren't so lucky we could be stuck here for days."

She hadn't really thought about that. So far, they were getting on fine, but once the small talk was exhausted, what then? He'd want to know about the restaurant, about Michael. "Finished?" When he nodded, she picked up the bowls and carried them to the sink. She caught sight of her face reflected in the window. A dark streak of dirt was on her cheek and her hair was a mess—she hadn't brushed it in twenty-four hours.

She ripped off a piece of kitchen roll and wiped her face. "Why didn't you tell me I've dirt all over my face? I better go take a shower."

"I didn't notice."

He didn't notice?

Fella twitched in the basket. Nick stood. "Go ahead—it's time for me to check on the patient."

FOUR

Summer dashed out of the room still rubbing at the mark on her face.

Nick crouched next to the basket. Fella was coming around. His eyes opened. It had been easy to see to his injuries while he was unconscious, but now the dog was awake Nick needed to act cautiously.

He let Fella sniff his hand, and puffed out a breath of relief when Fella licked his fingers. "Good boy." He stroked a hand over the dog's muzzle and head. "I think it's time to take out this cannula, don't you?" With his other hand he removed the connector of the drip from the dog's paw.

Fella showed no sign of aggression or fear—he was probably still too out of it to be fully aware.

Nick sat next to him and continued talking in the low, comforting tone that had earned him the nickname *pet whisperer* from those in the practice. He stroked Fella's head, shoulders and back to intensify the connection between them. To show the dog that he was friend, not foe. If three of them were going to be cooped up in this house for the next few hours or possibly days they all had to be friends.

Summer had dashed out of the room as though pursued by pack of wolves. Somehow he'd have to settle her nerves too. If only women were as easy to handle as dogs and cats. Stroking Summer... An erotic fantasy of stroking summer's long, tawny hair, smoothing his palm over her naked shoulders and back, came out of nowhere.

Shit. He could do with a shower too—a cold one.

Fella lifted his head off the floor, and stared at the door into the rest of the house.

A moment later, Summer walked in. She'd showered, washed and dried her hair, and put on makeup. A clean pair of jeans clung to her curves, and she'd pulled on a plain black sweatshirt. "He's awake?" Her eyes were wide. She clasped her hands together. "I can't believe he's letting you pet him."

"Come on over. Slowly."

He talked to Fella as Summer approached. She stopped a few feet away.

"Okay, now sit down, and scoot over." When she was close enough to touch, he reached for her hand. The touch of her skin made him want to close his fingers around hers, but he resisted the urge. "First we need to get him used to your smell."

She leaned forward and he brought her hand to Fella's nose. "This is Summer, Fella. She saved you."

Fella sniffed repeatedly. "Now, stroke him."

She scooted close, so close her body heat was almost tangible. Her scent drifted in the air, light and citrusy, she must have spritzed herself with cologne too.

Suddenly aware that he was sniffing her just as the dog was, Nick shifted a little further away.

She was talking to the dog now too, and he didn't seem to mind. The lack of aggression was heartening—he'd have a much better chance of being adopted if he could play nice with humans.

"I never believed he'd let me touch him," she murmured. "He's so dirty, though. Maybe we should wash him, or brush him or something."

"Right now, we just need to get him used to us. Make him comfortable in the house. He might never have been in a house before—I suspect they kept him chained outside."

Her fingers touched the ragged rope around Fella's neck. "I want to take this off."

Nick shook his head. "That can wait."

She withdrew her hand and stared into Nick's eyes. "I don't know how to thank you for all you've done. I bet the old vet wouldn't have even tried to drive out here with snow falling—"

"He didn't have the car for it."

"It's not about the car, it's about the man. You came. And we're both grateful. I have a larder full of provisions—we won't be eating fancy, but if we do get snowbound none of us will starve." She stood and walked to the packages he'd placed on the counter earlier. "I'll cook this chicken so we can feed it to Fella later."

Her heartfelt words had made warmth uncoil within him. "He shouldn't eat anything for a few hours, he's still woozy."

She ripped open the packet of chicken and dumped it in a saucepan. "Just water—don't go putting salt, pepper and herbs in there," he teased. Think Cordon Chien, rather than Cordon Bleu."

Fella made a noise, then threw up all over Nick's legs.

———

"EUWW." She could take most everything, but vomit... Summer turned away, every part of her trying to block out what had happened.

"Throw me that roll of kitchen paper and a trash bag, will you?" Nick asked.

She reached under the sink, found the things and handed them over, keeping herself well away from the mess. Fella'd mostly got Nick.

"Open the door for a second to clear the air—you don't have to stay in the room if it makes you nauseous too." He efficiently cleaned up the mess, then knotted the top of the bag. She stood back as he walked outside and dropped the bag into the rubbish bin. When he walked back inside, he looked down at his jeans. He'd cleared up as much as he could, but they were stained.

"I need to put these in the washing machine, pronto."

As she stood, Nick kicked off his shoes, undid each button of his jeans, eased them down, and shucked them off. She darned near swallowed her tongue—the guy had kilt-worthy legs. Firm, strong, muscular, with a dusting of dark hair.

"There's probably washing powder under the sink."

Her gaze shot up to his. Her jaw snapped shut.

Had he seen? The look on his face, all masculine swagger, hinted that he had. She'd been busted.

Caught staring at the impressive bulge in his tight, jersey boxers.

"Of course." She opened the cupboard—staying in there a couple of extra seconds until the heat that flooded her face cooled. "I guess that was the anesthetic."

"What?"

She straightened, holding a box of washing powder. "I said, I guess Fella was sick because of the anesthetic." The dog was quiet now, and seemed to have gone back to sleep.

"I reckon." Nick shoved his jeans into the washing machine, took the box of powder, and shook some into the dispenser. "I think I'll go shower."

"I'll find you something of Declan's." He wouldn't have taken all of his clothes to Spain, there'd be something in the drawers in his bedroom that would fit. Dressing Nick was a priority.

She let him go upstairs ahead of her though... after the day she'd had she deserved a little distraction.

In Declan's room, she found a couple of pairs of jeans, a few shirts and sweaters, and some socks. No underwear. Her brother had taken his entire collection with him. Summer wandered into her parents' room, and raided their father's drawers for a couple of pairs, which she placed on top of the pile.

She popped back into the bedroom to lay them out on the bed, but Nick'd had the quickest shower ever, and was standing in the middle of the bedroom with a towel wrapped around his waist.

Holy shit.

The rest of his body was just as impressive as the kilt-worthy legs. His chest was wide and muscled, and his abs looked hard enough to bounce nickels on. He was rubbing his hair with a towel. Once again, she fell under his spell, mesmerized by the flex of his biceps.

"I..."

He dropped the towel around his shoulders and looked over.

"I brought you some clothes."

"Oh, great." He took them from her, then frowned. "What are these, exactly?" He dangled a pair of her father's large, grey, undershorts from his finger.

"They're...um." *He knows what they are.* "They're my father's."

His expression probably matched her expression earlier—when the dog had thrown up.

"I won't be needing those." He handed them back. "I draw the line at wearing your father's underwear."

"Fair enough." She cast a last look at the deep grooves that cut from his hips downward. "I'll...um...I'll go and cook the chicken."

———

WELL, that was interesting.

Nick had known plenty of women, and he'd definitely seen that look before. The you're-so-hot-I'm-melting look. But he'd never seen it on Summer's face. She'd been flustered as he stripped in the kitchen, had waved him out of the door before her when they went upstairs, and he was pretty sure she'd been checking out his butt.

And his suspicion had been confirmed when she barged into the bedroom and caught him half-naked.

She'd tried to be surreptitious about it, but she was definitely checking him out.

He dried off and dressed; relieved Declan and he were the same size, so the clothes fit. Summer had given no explanation as to why she was in Brookbridge. Surely now must be the busy time for her restaurant? The head chef owner of Summer's Kitchen should be at home in London, providing delicious Christmas dinners and catering Christmas parties instead of boiling chicken for a sick dog.

And where was Mr. Polished? Maybe he still

had work to do. Maybe he was still in London shuffling people's money around. He was crazy to let her come over here alone.

He pulled on a clean pair of socks, and went downstairs.

"Would you like some more tea?"

The constant offering of tea was a deflection tactic. A way of shifting the mood to banal. She'd probably start talking about the weather in a moment.

Summer glanced out the window. "The snow is still..."

"Summer."

She turned.

"I don't want tea. It's gonna keep snowing out there for hours." He pulled out a chair and sat. "We are stuck here together—who knows for how long. We're going to have to get real here. No more superficial stuff."

Her chest rose and fell.

"Why aren't you in London?"

For a moment, he didn't think she would answer. She continued breathing heavily, fiddled with the sleeve of her sweater, and chewed in her bottom lip.

"Oh, crap." Giving in, she sat too. "I guess you're right." She rubbed her eyes. "I'm hiding out. No-one knows I'm here. But I guess you know that already, right? I knew the house would be empty, and we have keys, so I decided to camp out here for the holidays."

"What about the restaurant?"

"The restaurant...well, everything's fine there." She plastered on a smile, but it wasn't a convincing one. It was more like the sort of smile that someone would give having their picture taken while a gorilla stood on their foot. Forced. Insincere.

He just looked at her. Didn't say anything. When he and his brothers were kids, he'd always won staring contests. Had developed the useful skill of breaking someone down just by waiting.

Her smile wavered.

He waited.

"You don't believe me, do you?"

He waited some more.

"Okay." She shoved her hair back, twisted it into a rope and slung it over one of her shoulders. "I give up. I don't care if you believe me or not." Her eyes flashed in a rare display of temper. "Do you want to ask me anything else?"

"Where's Michael?"

She puffed out a breath. Closed her eyes, then opened them again. "Michael and I broke up. I haven't told anyone—my parents and Declan are on holiday. They don't need to know."

Her relationship had failed. As far as he knew,

Summer had never failed at anything important in her life. No wonder she was upset. But hiding out—keeping it secret...

"How long?" The night she'd opened the restaurant, Michael moved in to her apartment, demolishing Nick's half-baked plan of finally making a move, maybe asking her out for a date.

They'd been together for three years. A failed relationship must be tough, so close to the holidays. His longest relationship had lasted a few months—he'd had to end it when he realized she was thinking they'd be together forever.

Together forever and his name didn't belong in the same sentence.

She rubbed her hand over her eyes again, a look of exhausted resignation on her face. "I guess if I'm telling secrets, I should spill it all out there. Michael broke up with me four months ago."

Four months? She's kept this secret from her family for four months?

She stood up. "I've been up all night with that dog." She pointed to Fella snoring in his basket. "I'm going to sleep for a couple of hours."

FIVE

Summer climbed into bed fully dressed. She pulled the blankets up around her ears and curled into a fetal position. Even four months later, Michael's rejection hurt. A couple of good friends in London knew the truth—the whole story. They knew the truth about the restaurant.

When she'd been unable to pay the rent, Michael had asked her to move out. She just stared at him unable to believe what she was hearing.

"You're different," he'd said. "All you do is talk about your problems—you don't seem to have time for me anymore. I paid your share of the rent last month, but I can't continue to do that indefinitely. You must see that expecting me to support you is unrealistic."

"I don't expect you—"

"You do." He jiggled his car keys in his hand, moved from foot to foot, a restless flurry of activity. Any time they talked his body language revealed how he wanted to be anywhere but there. Anywhere but talking through their problems. "You've changed," he said again. "When we first moved in together you were confident, successful, fun."

Always the golden girl.

He looked at her with accusation written all over his face. Angry that she'd stepped off her pedestal to stand by his side. *What's the point?* He didn't want the real woman, the one plagued by doubts, facing real challenges.

He'd signed up as Ken to her Barbie. Lois to her Clark. Instead of supporting her when she was down, he wanted out. It was as though he'd gone to the cinema and bought a ticket to a rom-com and found himself in some deep psychological drama instead. Rather than sit through it, curious as to how the story might play out, he'd stomped to the box office and demanded his money back.

Summer groaned. Pulled the blanket up over her head to create a warm cocoon.

She'd been damned proud of the way she'd acted in response. She hadn't apologized. Hadn't explained. She'd packed up her things and put them in storage, and moved in to the room that served as office in the back of the restaurant. This holiday was to evaluate her future. Decide once and for all if now was the time to leave London, and try to build a new future in Ireland.

Explaining about Michael to Nick left her exhausted. Explaining to her family would be so much worse. There had been lies mixed in with the truth but she hadn't been able to face revealing the whole truth. Not yet.

SUMMER DREAMED she was on a sailboat, sliding across topaz glass. She pushed the tiller, and a sailor up front turned the wheel, taking them in different directions. A wind came out of nowhere, whipping the surface of the water into waves, tossing the little craft to and fro. *What's he doing?*

The sailor kept turning them into the wind.

She staggered forward, calling to him. Then made a lunge for the wheel.

The sail swung around, covered her face, she couldn't breathe...Summer woke up and peeled the sheet away from her face.

She'd recognized the sailor in her dream—the one who was sailing her in a direction she didn't want to go in—he was Nick.

Nick Logan thought he was in control of things.

Heck, most of the time, she had no doubt he was. Running a busy practice, having to make life and death decisions every day, meant he was blunt to the point of rudeness. If she didn't try to wrestle back some of that control, he'd have all her secrets out of her in no time. It was bad enough feeling pathetic; she didn't need to have it confirmed in heart-to-hearts with the Brookbridge vet.

And there was the subject of Declan. Her little brother was proud of the things she'd achieved. If she told Nick more of the story now, he might share the details with Declan.

She'd told him about Michael—the rest could wait. She didn't want to hide things from her family, but she didn't want to worry them either.

After washing her face, she went downstairs. The oven was on.

"What are you cooking?"

Nick looked up. "I put in some potatoes to bake about an hour ago."

"So—steaks, right?" She opened the fridge and retrieved them. "I have some broccoli and garlic. I'll make some garlic butter."

"About earlier…"

"Listen." She set the steaks on the table. Rested the knuckles of both hands on the smooth wood, and brought her head level to his. "I was touchy. Let's forget it."

He opened his mouth to speak.

"No. Seriously. I don't want to talk about any personal stuff. I just don't. When I said let's forget it, I meant it. We can talk about you, about movies, about books, about your work, heck, we can even watch wildlife documentaries and talk about Attenborough. I don't care."

"That's presuming the power stays on."

"So are we okay about the conversation earlier?"

"What conversation?" Nick opened a bottle of red wine, and poured two glasses. "I've forgotten."

Summer grabbed a couple of onions from vegetable rack. Then she took out a chopping board and a lethal looking knife. She peeled, then sliced them into thin rounds.

"I'm going to feed Fella now." Nick had already prepared a bowl with the cooled chicken. He walked to the dog and placed it on the floor beside him. Fella stirred, and managed to sit up. "Take it easy there." Nick pushed the bowl right up to the basket. Fella sniffed it, then started to eat. "Slow down."

Fella paid no heed, eating so fast he didn't appear to be chewing at all.

"He's starving." Summer paused in her chopping to watch the dog. He had finished the meat and lapped up all the liquid. He struggled up to standing, stepped out of the basket, and licked it clean. The metal bowl clanged against the wooden floorboards as he pushed it around with his nose.

When he finished, Fella looked up at Nick with hope that there may be more.

"That's it." Nick opened his hands wide, and Fella sniffed them. "You want to go out?"

"He won't be able to make it outside, will he?"

Nick walked to the back door, opened it and peered out. "It's stopped snowing. Come on, Fella." He smacked his thigh, encouraging the dog to limp to him. It was a tortuous process. Fella staggered and weaved partly as the aftermath of the anesthetic and partly as a result of his injury.

Nick stuck his feet into a pair of wellingtons he'd found at the back door and stepped outside. "Come on, Fella."

Nick pulled the door closed.

Summer melted butter and olive oil in a heavy frying pan and fried the onions.

She hammered the steaks, seasoned them, and put them under the grill. *Where's the steamer?* A search through her mother's cupboards came up empty—she made a mental note to buy one and leave it here as a present—so she put water on to boil to cook the broccoli.

It was good to be cooking again. Since the restaurant went bust, she'd lost her enthusiasm for cooking. It was hardly worth cooking for one.

The door eased open accompanied by a blast of cold air. "Success," Nick said. Fella trailed in his wake and once inside made straight for the basket. "That smells amazing. I love fried onions."

"Who doesn't?" Evie probably made them for him every time they ate steak.

"Any time I'm cooking I forget how much I love fried onions. I always forget to buy them. I guess that's the difference between an amateur and a professional. What are you doing now?" He stood close, watching her with interest.

She peeled some garlic cloves and crushed them with the side of the knife. "Making garlic butter."

"Why aren't you chopping them?"

Cooking lessons for beginners. "Crushing garlic first is the best way to release the oils. I crush it first and then chop it." She snipped a few leaves of parsley from the pot she'd placed on the windowsill when she came back from the shop. "I like to add some parsley to it as well." She whipped up some butter and added the garlic and chopped parsley.

"It never seems worth making all these extras when it's just me. I mean look, you even remember to buy parsley—I've never bought parsley in my life."

It's just him? The relationship with Evie couldn't be that serious if she didn't live with him, or cook for him very often. "Well the trick is to make a little bit more than you need, roll it into a little log in saran wrap, and keep it in the door of the fridge. Then it'll be there when you need it the next time. You can even freeze it."

"Hmm." Nick took off his boots and coat. "More wine?

"Sure."

He placed a full glass of wine next to the chopping board. "Maybe you can give me a few pointers cooking-wise. By a cruel twist of fate, I'm making Christmas dinner this year."

"Don't you usually go to your parents' for Christmas dinner?"

Nick sat on the chair nearest the wood-burning stove and crossed his feet at the ankles. "Ah, that's with a cruel twist of fate comes in. My mother hurt her arm a couple of weeks ago. She got into a complete panic, flustered because the entire family is coming home for Christmas. I was *trying* to reassure her." He scowled.

"What happened?"

"Well, I started to give her a pep talk. You know the one—the you-can-do-anything you-put-your-mind-to talk."

"Because you're a strong, independent woman?" She grinned.

Nick nodded. "That's the one. Anyway, it backfired big-time. I guess I overdid it when I said she cooked dinner every night, cooking Christmas dinner would be easy. Her eyes flashed and she told me it wasn't easy."

"Uh-oh."

"I disagreed, and she said 'if you think it's so damn easy why don't you do it?' I thought she was joking—Ma never lets anyone into her kitchen. But apparently she was serious. Every time I see her I keep waiting for her to relent, but she just keeps asking if I'm going to do turkey or goose, have I made the Christmas pudding yet..."

"How many are coming?"

Nick counted on his fingers. "Me, the parents, Matthew, his wife April, my brother from New York, Amy, Finn and Val—Jesus, that's nine. I don't suppose you'd like to join us, would you?"

"Nick Logan, are you trying to palm off a cooking job onto me?"

He looked so pained she couldn't help but giggle.

"Hey, you can't blame me. An award-winning chef lands in my lap the week before Christmas, it must be a sign."

"What about Evie, surely she can help."

"Evie?" He looked puzzled. "Why on earth would Evie help?"

"You called her to let her know you won't be home tonight. I thought..."

Nick sipped his wine. "I called her so my colleagues would know where I am. Evie is the receptionist. I don't have anyone waiting at home for me. I'm just as single as you are."

———

THE MORE HE thought about it, the better idea it seemed. "What was your plan? Were you thinking of just cooking something for one, this Christmas?"

"That is still my plan." She flipped the steaks, and put two plates into the oven to warm. "Unlike you, I shall be having a ready meal."

"A ready meal? What, you mean one of those pre-prepared things from the freezer? My usual fare?"

"Yup. I decided on crispy duck for one. The only food preparation I'll be doing is chopping a cucumber."

She sounded serious.

"In that case, I shall make it my mission to persuade you to change your mind. My apartment is the size of a shoebox, so I'm moving home on Christmas Eve so I can be up early to start cooking. I've ordered a turkey. A fifteen pounder. How difficult can it be?"

"It's not so much the cooking, it's the timing. There are so many different things to prepare, you need to make a plan." She took the potatoes out of the oven and plated their dinner.

He stood and put the silverware onto the table. She set a plate of beautifully cooked food in front of him.

He started to eat. The steak was medium, just the way he liked it. Garlic butter glistened on top. The onion rings were light brown and slightly crispy around the edges. The inside of the potatoes was fluffy, and the broccoli was firm rather than mushy.

"God, this is delicious."

"Timing. If I timed it wrong the vegetables would be overcooked. The last thing you want is overcooked sprouts with your Christmas lunch. There are some things you can prepare in advance. I've got a great recipe for cranberry sauce—"

"I have a jar of that."

She pulled a face. "My homemade cranberry and orange sauce with port in is easy—you can make it up a few days in advance and it'll knock their socks off. I'll write down the recipe."

Messing about making stuff when it was readily available in the supermarket sounded like a waste of time. "I thought I'd just make the absolute basics—I can buy a lot of things ready-made and just heat them up."

"Well, you *could.*" The expression on her face

indicated she wasn't impressed by his plan. "Or you could take the view that this is your chance to show your mother that you can produce a fantastic meal. After all, you told her it was easy."

Me and my big mouth. "I meant it was easy for her—she cooks all the time. I didn't mean it would be easy for everyone. I anticipate it's going to be bloody difficult for me."

She refilled his wine glass and topped up her own. "Nick Logan, I'm surprised at you. I thought you were a can-do guy." There was a hint of tease in her voice.

"What gave you that idea?"

She sipped her wine. "Well, let's see..." She thought for a moment. "I remember a summer in Dingle."

The memory of the vacation in Dingle formed in his mind—one long ago summer. Declan and Summer had been allowed to ask a friend each to join them in the cottage they'd rented for a couple of weeks in Castlegregory. He couldn't remember the name of the friend Summer asked along, but he had been Declan's choice—they'd been inseparable since they met at aged eight.

"I was eighteen, so you were much younger," Summer said. "We went surfing out on the Maharees, don't you remember?"

The huge, white sand dunes of the peninsula.

Four of them bundled up against the Irish summer chill in wetsuits. She'd been a goddess in black rubber.

Even then, he'd mooned about after her like a lovesick puppy.

"You taught me to surf." Her voice was dreamy. "You stood me on a surfboard on the sand. You were so sweet."

Nick grimaced. Sweet. What a crappy word. "I'd done it before." He'd always loved surfing. Being out in nature, sailing across the surface of the water.

"And you told me something like, 'You can do it, you can do anything.' When we went back out, you held the side of my board, and we surfed back to shore. That was the first time I managed to get up on the board. It was only for a moment, but I did it. I did it because of you."

It was amazing how she remembered it all so differently. "Don't you remember what happened before you reached the shore?" Nick gritted his teeth. He didn't think he'd ever forget it.

"I remember getting a mouthful of salty water, and floundering on the sand like a beached seal. You picked me up. Everyone laughed. I was mortified."

"You deflected their laughter easily enough."

"Did I?" Her forehead wrinkled, had she really forgotten the cruel words she'd spoken? The way she'd shouted that he should take his hands off her?

She smiled. "You were always such a sweet kid."

"I wasn't a kid. Your friend wanted me to kiss her that holiday, did she ever tell you?"

Her eyes widened. "Sharon tried to kiss you?"

Sharon, yes, that was her name.

"I'm so sorry, she never should have done that—she was so much older than you, I'm appalled. I never knew." She looked at him over the rim of her wineglass. "Did you?"

"Did I what?"

"Did you kiss her?"

He put down his knife and fork. "I was sixteen, not twelve. There's only two years between us, Summer. So yes, I damn well did. Even though there'd been someone else I wanted to kiss that holiday. I wanted to kiss you."

SIX

"That's crazy." She never thought she'd be having this discussion with her brother's best friend. He'd been a good-looking kid, but...Summer shook her head. He'd been a kid. Just like her brother.

"Yeah, well, it was a long time ago." Nick finished the rest of his dinner and pushed his plate away. "I guess I wasn't the only one. Most of my class had the hots for you back then."

"I used to get valentine cards from some of Declan's friends," she said. "But never from you."

"Declan would have killed me. You were off limits."

"Funny, isn't it? Looking back." She couldn't help wondering when that crush had withered. Now she was thirty-two and he was thirty, the years between them were nothing. "If I met you for the first time today, I wouldn't even know you were younger than me."

"What would you do, if this was our first meeting?" His direct gaze pierced her. "If I'd come out here to help with Fella, and you'd never met me before, how would things be different?"

The conversation was moving into uncharted territory. The temptation to flirt was strong, but she tamped it down, and tried to answer honestly.

"I guess I'd be making small talk. I'd be nervous, stuck alone in a house with a man I didn't know. I'd be hoping you didn't make any sudden moves."

He grinned. "Well, you know me, so there's no need to worry." He stood, picked up the plates, and stacked them next to the dishwasher. "I'm going to sleep in here tonight—keep an eye on Fella." He waved at the old sofa that had previously lived in the sitting room, but had been moved into the kitchen when the new suite of furniture arrived. "That will do me fine. Tomorrow morning we'll assess the situation, and with luck we can drive back down to Brookbridge."

He shoved his hands into the front pocket of his jeans. "I'll grab a quilt and pillow off Declan's bed." With that, he walked out of the room.

The revelation that he'd wanted to kiss her so many years ago, opened a door in her mind that she'd never noticed before. She'd been a success to most everyone, all through her life, but memories bombarded her now of the times that she'd failed.

The day on the beach. That time she had too much to drink at a school dance, and fallen, ripping her hose on the gravel. Both times, Nick had been there—had witnessed her humiliation, and helped her up.

Outside the dance, he'd helped her onto a bench, had turned away while she slid off her hose, and had wiped the blood from her knees with a tissue he found in her bag. Even then, he was caring for injured creatures.

When he'd stripped earlier, she'd been knocked off her feet by a wave of lust. All thoughts of who he was, their history, had been churned up, like sand in seafoam. Now, the memories of Nick merged with the reality of who he was now. A man she found attractive. An available man, who at one time had found her attractive too.

She poured the last of the wine into her glass and drained it. Nick wouldn't hurt her, wouldn't judge her, and it had been so long since she'd had a man's arms around her...what happened in a snowstorm, stayed in a snowstorm, didn't it?

———

SO, that happened.

He'd made a complete idiot of himself with Summer. Had confessed a teenage crush, which still seemed to be very much alive, if his body's reaction to her was anything to go by. Talking to her —hearing her reminisce about that vacation in Kerry, had re-awoken sensations long buried. He remembered it all in vivid Technicolor. Summer in her white bikini, wriggling into the wetsuit, and him holding the board in front to hide the evidence that merely the sight of her gave him an erection.

The look in her eyes when he picked her up from the churning surf. Grateful for a moment, and then horrified as the others laughed. She'd brushed his hands away and loudly shouted, "Get off me!" as though he was attacking her or something.

He'd been the embarrassed one then.

Declan had tried to say she was just being like that because she couldn't bear to fail, but Nick felt a fool, being turned on like that. The incident hadn't killed his feelings for Summer, but had made him cautious.

And by the time he built up the courage to try again, she belonged to someone else.

Since then he'd made a decision, conscious or not, to never let a woman tangle with his emotions.

Now he felt like he was back there...worse, that

he was in deep water, in danger of getting dragged into the undertow.

Jesus, get a grip. Nothing had changed. She was still Declan's sister. She had a life in London, a successful restaurant to go back to. And hearing that he'd had a crush back then had come as a total surprise. *Don't be weird. Just act natural.* He snatched up Declan's quilt and pillow and stomped downstairs.

She'd cleared away the dinner things by the time he walked back into the room, and was sitting at the table. "I thought we could play cards." She held up a deck. "I guess we could watch TV, but I don't want to leave the warmth."

"I haven't played cards for years," he said. "And from what I remember, you're a bit of a card shark. You used to fleece me and Declan."

"Okay, you choose the game then." Her mouth curved in a smile.

He eyed her carefully. "Poker's your game, isn't it?"

He had a distinct memory of her winning a trophy for a poker tournament while she was in college.

She held up her hands. "Busted. Yeah, I won a couple of years in a row."

"In that case, I choose snap."

She snorted. "Snap? Who plays snap? That's a child's game."

"It's a game we both have an equal chance of winning. Do you want to play for money? I have a few euros..."

"Euros." Her lip curled. "Come on, we can do better than that." She'd cleared away the wine as well, and had put two shot glasses and a bottle of whisky on the table. "Shots." She poured a measure into his glass and then her own. "Every time you lose a game, you have to take a shot."

He could drink most people under the table. "Okay, you're on."

She tucked a strand of hair behind her ear. "Or lose a piece of clothing."

Nick felt his eyes widen. "You want to play strip snap? With snow outside?"

She chewed her bottom lip. "I guess that's a stupid idea. Let's forget it." She shuffled the cards, looking down rather than at him.

What messages was she sending? If it had been anyone else but Summer, he'd think there was some flirtation going on here. He tested the waters. "If you want to see me naked, you only have to ask."

Her gaze shot up. "I almost did already."

"Almost asked?"

"Almost saw you naked." She cut the deck and

started to deal. "Upstairs, earlier. I just thought we could make playing cards more fun."

She was a study in awkward, although she was hiding it well. She picked at the end of her sleeve, tugging the wool down at her wrist. Tucked a stand of hair behind her ear. Rubbed the nape of her neck.

"I can think of nothing more fun than winning every hand and seeing you naked," he said without the trace of a smile. "But I'm not about to risk hypothermia." He picked up the pile of cards. "Let's play."

She won the first game, shouting snap and slamming her hand down on the cards so enthusiastically he laughed. "You really can't bear to lose, can you?"

"What can I say, I have an over-developed sense of competition." She gestured to the shot glass of whisky. "Drink."

He swallowed the amber liquid in one swallow. "Let's go again."

The same thing happened for the next game. He drank another shot. "If we were playing for clothing, I guess I'd be down to my jeans and socks by now."

"Wouldn't you lose your socks first?" She tilted her head to the side.

Flirting.

"Socks would be the last thing to go. You've gotta keep your feet warm." He leaned across the table and stared into her eyes. "I can't help thinking you're trying to get me drunk."

"Why would I do that?" Her eyes sparkled. Her chin angled up. *Definitely flirting.*

"I don't know. Maybe you find me irresistible, and want to lower my inhibitions."

"That would make me a very calculating older woman."

He picked her glass up and handed it over. "You should drink one too. So both of us lose our inhibitions at the same rate."

She swallowed the shot and spluttered. "What could that lead to?"

What indeed? "We're alone. Anything could happen—if you want it to."

She sucked on her bottom lip, her mind definitely running over the possibilities. "This is crazy, you're Declan's best friend."

"You think of me like a brother." A knot formed in his stomach. He forced himself to consider the truth—that she didn't want him, couldn't get past the brothersfriendzone...

"No. I never thought of you like that." She tossed a card down on the table. "I always thought you were sort of hot, but, you know...you were younger."

"Age doesn't matter."

"Not now, but when you were seventeen it sure did."

"You thought I was hot when I was seventeen?" He threw a card down on the table.

"I did. I admit it." She threw a card down too, followed by her hand on top. "Snap."

"I always thought you were gorgeous."

Her eyes widened.

"I still do."

She put down her cards, stood up, leaned over the table and kissed him square on the mouth.

———

SHE TASTED OF WHISKY. The kiss was an impulsive thing, over in a moment. She pulled back and smiled as though it hadn't been anything, hadn't meant anything.

Forget that. "You call that a kiss?" He really shouldn't take it further, but there was no way he could pretend it was nothing. He'd dreamed of kissing her for years. Really kissing her, not just the quick touch of closed mouths.

"This is how I'd kiss you."

She didn't move, didn't look away. Her lips parted and awareness was in her eyes, awareness that maybe she'd poked a snake. Teased, without assessing the consequences.

He stood. Walked around the table. Slipped a hand behind her nape, and brought his mouth a millimeter away from hers. Her pupils expanded. Her eyelids dipped, but she still watched him. He breathed in the scent of her—heady, arousing. "If you want me to stop, tell me now."

She stayed silent.

Nick teased her lips with his. Traced the seam of them with his tongue, then angled his head and poured all the long years of wanting into his kiss. He'd meant to make a point, to show she couldn't just kiss him and sit back down as though nothing had happened. But the moment she opened her mouth and started to kiss him back, his ability to think clearly evaporated.

Her hands were on his chest, tugging his sweater, demanding he get closer.

He snaked his other hand around her narrow waist, kissing her as if there would be no tomorrow —would be no consequences of their actions. As if nothing in the world existed but the two of them and this moment. Their mouths parted for a split second, then she moaned and started to kiss him again—as though she was just as intoxicated and mesmerized by the taste of him as he was of her.

Intoxicated. Shit. Intoxicated. He pulled away. Just how much of that wine had she drunk?

Her eyes flickered open. "Nick?" Her cheeks were rosy, and the fevered light in them could be desire, or could be something else, could be alcohol induced.

"Not like this." His hands dropped to his sides and he took a step back.

And then the lights went out.

SEVEN

Summer could see Nick's outline, but nothing more. She swayed, trying to make sense of what had occurred in the last few moments. She'd been touched by his words—flattered with the idea that he thought she was gorgeous, especially as she'd looked like the creature from the black lagoon when he arrived.

A shadow of the boy he'd been was in his eyes—the boy who hadn't laughed like the others, but had run his hands down her arms when he picked her up from the sand. Disturbed by his touch, thrown off-kilter by the warmth in his eyes, she'd overreacted.

She hadn't owned it, but she couldn't forget how she'd pushed him away and diverted attention from her humiliation. For a mad moment, she'd been thrust back to that time. She'd kissed him, not just because of his words, but because she remembered what a bitch she'd been back then.

An apology, of sorts, but he'd sure turned that on its head. The moment he touched her, electricity zinged through her, silencing her voice and frying her synapses. And that kiss...her bones melted at the memory of it. The taste of him was still in her mouth. Her fingers itched to touch him again. But he'd pulled away just before the lights went out...

"We need a torch. Or candles." He was back to being Mr. Organized, while she stood, still stunned by the effect of his kiss. "Summer. Focus."

She shimmied her head. "There's a torch under the sink, and candles on the dresser." With her hands out in front of her she shuffled forward until she found the edge of the table. "I'll get the candles."

She fumbled to the dresser, located the tealights in candleholders that always lived there, and sent silent thanks to her absent mother for being so organized that a box of matches nestled next to them.

By the time she had them lit, a flashlight's beam was playing across the room.

"It might be a fuse." Nick jerked open the

fridge. "No, the sockets are out as well. We have no power."

Outages were common whenever there was a storm, so she was inclined to agree. "Damn, they're not likely to fix it quickly with the snow..." Her mind raced. "The heating system won't work, or the pump for the water."

She carried two candles to the table.

"You should go up and fill the bath," Nick said. "I'll build up the wood burning stove, and bring in some more wood."

"I saw water bottles in the storeroom earlier." There were bound to be more candles in there too. She picked up the candle from the table and went to look. As she filled them at the sink, Nick trekked out to the woodshed with the wheelbarrow.

The blast of air from the open door was frigid so she closed it behind him. The house was warm now, but wouldn't remain so for long.

The dog whined. "Calm down, Fella." She dropped another couple of tea-lights into jam jars that she'd found in the storeroom and lit them. "Everything will look better in the morning."

———

HE'D DONE the best he could for tonight. They had water, and the wood stove was fully fuelled.

Summer had headed up to bed a couple of hours ago. She'd been quiet since the lights went out. Unusually quiet. Probably regretting the foolish impulse that had made her kiss him. He should have just let it be, but impulse control where Summer was concerned was a problem. He remembered the look in her eyes, the dawning awareness. When he'd kissed her, for a moment she hadn't responded.

But then she'd kissed him back with such passion all his misgivings had disappeared in an instant.

He was no monk. There were some fine looking women in Brookbridge—many of whom he'd dated at some time or another. But he'd never been aroused as quickly as he had with Summer. Maybe it was because he'd spent so many years craving her.

He'd crawled onto the sofa fully dressed under Declan's duvet, and had spent the last while trying to get comfortable. The damn thing was too short— his feet hung over the ends. And a spring or two had broken in the middle, making it damn uncomfortable.

If he had to stay here for another night it would be in Declan's bed.

Fella would have to deal with being alone. There was nothing wrong with being alone—Nick preferred his solitude, didn't really like sharing space with anyone. But the thought of sharing a bed tonight with the woman upstairs was appealing.

If she wasn't drunk.

Stop thinking about her. He closed his eyes and willed himself to sleep.

A couple of hours later he shot up in bed—heart pounding.

A long, mournful howl.

Fella. Nick clambered off the sofa and re-lit the candle. "It's okay, Fella."

The dog looked back at him, tilted his head to the side, then pointed his nose at the ceiling and howled again.

What the hell? There was no aggression in the dog's body language, he sat in the basket rather than standing, and his hackles weren't rising. "Shush." A sound came from upstairs, a high-pitched, discordant sound.

He picked up the candle and walked to the bottom of the stairs. The sound was louder—more distinct. Was she... Was she *singing?*

An answering howl came from the kitchen.

Nick pushed up his sleeve and checked his watch. Four-twenty. It was four-twenty in the goddamn morning and Summer and the dog were having a karaoke session. *Jesus.* He tramped up the stairs and pushed open the bedroom door.

She lay in bed with eyes closed. Earbuds hung

from her ears and she was singing at the top of her voice. He couldn't fault her music choice—heck, everyone loves the Foo Fighters—but she was murdering *The Best Of You*.

She was wearing fleecy pajamas and a wooly hat, and had a blanket around her shoulders and the covers pulled up as high as possible around her chest. Her head tilted side to side, keeping pace with the music. Her hands rose from the coverlet, and her wrists rotated as she mimed the drum solo.

"Summer."

She kept singing, and the tinny sound of music bled from the earbuds. There was no way she could hear him over that.

He knew the song well—she was only halfway through. He could walk over and tap her on the arm, which might cause a heart attack, or worse still, a scream...or he could wait until she finished and then speak in the silence at the song's end.

He propped a shoulder on the doorjamb and waited.

———

SHE NEVER SHOULD HAVE GONE to sleep that afternoon. In the months after the double disasters of losing first the restaurant and then

Michael, she'd been plagued with insomnia, and resorted to sleeping pills.

It had taken the help of a doctor to break the habit—she couldn't add the shame of having become addicted to sleeping pills to her trophy cabinet of failures. She'd built up a careful routine —hot bath, warm cocoa, never napping in the day— to get her over it.

And then she'd blown it by sleeping in the day, and not having any of her usual tricks to fall back on. So she'd read for a while on her backlit Kindle, tried lying there, mentally counting sheep, and given up when the vision of sheep had been replaced by visions of Nick, wearing just a towel, leaping over hurdles.

Every leap, she imagined his towel falling off.

It wasn't working. So she'd plugged her earphones into her phone, and dialed up her favorite playlist. There was nothing soothing about it, but at least listening made her feel better.

The music faded.

"Summer!"

Her eyelids shot open—a crazy drum-solo crashing in her chest.

Nick walked toward her. She pulled out the earbuds and flicked off the music.

"You were singing." He dropped down on the side of the bed. "Really loudly."

"So loudly I woke you up?" She loved singing, but had such a terrible voice she never did it when someone could hear. Apart from now. "How long have you been standing there?"

"A couple of minutes. I did try to get your attention, but..." He shrugged. "I reckoned I better wait."

"So you heard everything." Every uninhibited yowl. And he'd seen her air-drumming too. She wrinkled her nose. "I'm sorry I woke you."

"You didn't wake me. At least not directly. You have a fan downstairs. Fella does an awesome howlalong." He rubbed his arms. "Christ, it's cold in here." He stood. Then he looked at the little white box in her hands. "That's not your phone, is it?"

"Of course it is." Her music collection lived on her smartphone, there seemed little point in doubling up with a dedicated device.

"It's off now, right?"

She looked down.

"We have no power. When the battery runs out..."

She covered her mouth with her hand. "Crap, I didn't think of that."

He yawned. "I'm going back down." He turned at the door. "Get some sleep."

"Well, I would if I could." She couldn't keep the

edge of snark from her voice. "Sorry, I know I woke you and Fella, but I have insomnia, I've been trying to go to sleep for hours."

He rubbed the back of his head. His hair was standing up all over the place; he was rumpled and sleepy, and appealing as hell. Bed head looked sexy on him—at least she didn't have to share what it looked like on her. She pulled the wooly hat down a fraction over her ears.

He exhaled. "Do you want to come downstairs and have something hot to drink?" He didn't exactly roll his eyes, but she was pretty sure he was holding one back.

"Yes. I would." She swung her legs out of bed, shoved her fluffy socks into Ugg knockoffs, and wrapped the blanket around herself. "That might help."

And if not, at least she'd have something attractive to look at.

It was warm downstairs. Fella looked up as they entered, and wagged his tail. "Oh, look! He's pleased to see us!" She trotted over to give him a pat on the head.

"I'll bring in some more logs." He grabbed some from the wheelbarrow outside the back door and trudged to the stove.

She filled a saucepan with water, and put it to heat. "You're joining me?"

Nick grunted. "Okay, maybe. I guess." He rubbed his eyes. "Actually, no. I don't think I can face tea right now." He lay down on the sofa and threw the blanket over himself. His long legs stretched, extending past the ends. "You must have been uncomfortable." A twinge of guilt. She would fit on the sofa easily, and seeing as she had little chance of sleep... "Would you like to go upstairs? You could slip into my bed and I'll stay down here."

His eyes were dark in the shadowy light from the candle. "No point. It'll be dawn soon." He yawned. "If we're still here tomorrow night, I'll sleep in Declan's bed."

She padded over to fetch a cup and a teabag, crossed to the fridge and fetched the milk. The water was simmering on the top of the wood-burning stove, so she took it off and made the tea. "Look...about before." She added milk, then walked back to return the carton to the fridge. "I remember more about that day at the beach than I admitted." She couldn't look at him. "I was a real bitch that day." She picked a spoon out the drawer and flicked the teabag into the sink. "I'm sorry."

Confession made, she took a deep breath and turned.

Nick's eyes were closed. His chest moved up and down in a regular rhythm.

"Seriously?" She snuggled down in the

armchair opposite, tucked the blanket over herself, and watched him sleep.

Her own sleep was elusive, and by the time the darkness lifted with the arrival of a watery dawn, she'd given up hope of it and decided to face the day instead. She blew out the candle, and threw a couple of logs into the stove. Then she wandered to the window and looked out.

Snow. As far as the eye could see. Nick's land rover was covered in a thick frosting, and all signs of their footsteps from the day before were buried.

She changed into rubber boots and went outside to investigate further.

At least today the wind had died down. The scene was a pretty picture postcard—but freezing. She wrapped the blanket around herself and shivered. Branches of the oaks and beeches were weighed down with heavy snow. Beneath her feet, the snow was crispy, leaving distinct edges in her footsteps. There was no way they would get down to the village through this. Which meant there was no chance of getting the electricity supply restored during the day.

Her sigh puffed out white vapor in the clear air.

What can I cook, with only a wood-burning stove? She did a mental inventory of the ingredients she'd brought. Something all in one pan, there wouldn't be space on the top for more than that.

Maybe a soup. Or a stew. If there was any danger of the food spoiling in the refrigerator, she could store it outside—it was as cold as the inside of a fridge out here.

Retracing her steps, she opened the door again. Nick was snoring softly on the sofa, contorted into an unnatural position.

Fella looked up, and got to his feet.

"Come on, Fella," she said.

He'd been cooped up all night, he must need to go outside, and he'd managed fine last night when Nick took him out.

The dog walked stiff legged from his basket, stretched and yawned. "So you were singing along with me last night, were you?" She patted his head as he cleared the door.

Seb had been a part of her family forever, but she hadn't owned a pet since then. She'd spent every available hour at the restaurant, and owning a dog or cat had seemed selfish, as she would rarely be there.

Fella sniffed around the base of a tree and lifted a leg. "Good boy." In such a short time, she'd become attached to him. Maybe it was because she'd saved him—if he'd been left in the woodshed overnight, starved and listless, he would have died. Maybe it was because she could do with a companion to ease the loneliness of the past few months. Would he find a home easily? She hoped so. He was sniffing in the bushes now. "Time to go back in."

The tips of her fingers were going white. "Fella."

He ignored her. Then let out a bark.

A rabbit popped out of a hole half hidden by snow at the side of the little clump of bushes and ran off into the woods.

"Fella!" The dog took off after it in hot pursuit.

EIGHT

Nick woke to the sound of frantic shouting.

He propelled himself from under the quilt. Fella was gone. Summer's voice—*outside.* He ran to the door and tugged it open.

Summer was shouting, staring out across the field.

"What the hell's going on?"

"Oh, Nick—" She ran to him and grabbed his arm. "It's Fella. He saw a rabbit and took off after it. I didn't think he would be able to run, but...but..."

"I get it. Come on." He grabbed her hand and tugged her toward the house.

She resisted. "We have to go after him!"

"There's no way you're chasing a dog wearing that." He looked down at her pajamas. "Pull on your jeans and jumper and put on a coat." He sounded like someone's mother. Shit, he sounded like his own mother. But the air was so cold it stung his cheeks. He would be sensible, even if she wasn't. "Which way did he go?"

There were inside now, and he shoved his arms into his coat.

"Across the field toward the river." She was already heading for the stairs. "I'll follow you."

Nick picked up his car keys from the counter. He always carried a dog whistle in his glove compartment. Armed with the whistle, he took off in the direction Fella had gone, running as fast as was possible in the thick snow. Fella's tracks and the tiny footprints of the rabbit preceding him. "Fella!" He picked up pace. This much exercise could rip open Fella's stitches—he needed to get the dog back inside as soon as possible. He shoved his keys into his pocket as he ran. There. In the distance he made out the loping form of the dog, heading straight for the river.

At least rabbits don't swim...He blew a short blast through the whistle, and slowed down as Fella stopped and turned. "Come back here, you stupid bloody animal!" he shouted.

Fella looked away and kept going.

"Shit." Nick ran again and as he got closer blew the whistle again.

Fella was on the riverbank. At the alien sound, he whipped around. His paws skittered on the icy bank, a macabre slapstick move like those seen in old black and white movies, and then he slipped, and hit the water.

"Fella!" Summer's shout was behind him as Nick rushed to the riverbank.

The current was fast flowing; Fella's eyes were wide and frantic as he struggled to make it back to the bank.

"Oh crap." Nick shed his coat, toed off his boots, and dived in after him.

The water was so cold he couldn't catch his breath. And flowing so fast, swimming against it was near impossible.

"What are you doing! You..." She was screaming stuff he couldn't understand, couldn't waste time listening to. Instead, Nick struck out to Fella. He managed to get a hand around the rope that still hung around Fella's neck, and pulled him close.

With the oversized dog clamped to his side, he struck out to the bank with the other.

"Here!" Summer had knelt, wrapping her ankles through the broken trunk of a thorn tree by the water's edge. She held out her hand, fingers wide.

Somehow he made it to her. She grabbed his

hand, and, her face, red and sweating with the effort, pulled him and Fella to safety.

For a long moment, the three of them lay prostrate on the frozen blades of grass, breathing heavily.

Then she untangled her legs from the tree trunk, and stumbled up to standing.

"You need to get inside. You both need to get inside. Come on." She grasped his hand.

"In a minute." His heart was still pounding from the effort. His legs were jelly; he doubted that they could hold him.

"Nick." She leaned down and stared into his face. "You have to move. If you stay out here you'll get hypothermia."

Fella struggled to his feet, a sad, sorry excuse for a dog. He sniffed Nick's face.

Dog breath.

"Okay, okay." Nick sat then managed to get to his feet. With his entire body shaking, he staggered after her across the field to the house.

———

NICK'S SKIN WAS PALE—CLAMMY to the touch. He stood in the middle of the warm kitchen, shaking uncontrollably. His fingers fumbled with his clothes.

"Try to get your clothes off." She took the stairs two at a time, racing to the bathroom where she grabbed two large towels. By the time she sped back to him, he had managed to rid himself of the sopping sweater and T-shirt. He was trying to unbutton his jeans. "Let me." She shoved a towel into his hands and dropped the other on the kitchen table. "Dry your chest."

Her fingers unbuttoned the snap at his waist, then she unzipped him, and slid down his jeans.

Commando.

She breathed slow and steady, and tried not to react at the sight of Nick's nakedness. The poor guy had enough to deal with without her embarrassment.

"Lift your leg." He did so, and she freed him from first one leg of his jeans then the other. She stripped off his soaking socks, and grabbed the other towel from the table and wrapped it around him, rubbing vigorously to try and get his circulation going—to heat his body.

His crotch—she just patted. Then she stretched up, and rubbed his back, and over the curve of his butt while he dried his cock and balls. In a few moments, he was dry, but still so cold he could freeze water just by sticking a finger in it.

"Get under the blanket." She pushed him to the sofa, and draped the blanket over him.

Then she turned to Fella and rubbed his fur dry with the towel.

"Into your basket, Fella."

He did as she asked, and she draped a dry towel over him. The heat of the woodstove would soon warm him. Nick however...

His face was still white, and his lips were going blue. *Body to body.* She'd seen a documentary about polar explorers, about what they had to do in cases of hypothermia. Nothing heated the body quicker than skin on skin contact.

"Hold on." She stripped off her sweater and removed her jeans. Then she pulled back the cover and plastered her warm body against his.

She gritted her teeth as her bra pressed against his chest. Wrapped her arms around back and pressed her stomach to his. She wound her leg over his frigid thigh and ran her hands over his back, again and again. "You'll warm up soon."

He was too cold to even smile, but his lips moved in a poor imitation of one. "I didn't think," he whispered.

"Damn right, you didn't think." She rubbed his side, his thigh, the top of his butt. "You're crazy, do you know that?" Her heart had almost stopped when she'd seen him dive into the water. She'd feared she'd lose both of them. And it wasn't the prospect of having to explain to their parents why

Nick Logan had lost his life in the river that made her frantic. It was the thought of never seeing his smile again. Never hearing him bossing her around. "If I'd lost you I'd have..." She bit back tears. Crying all over him wouldn't help. She pressed her face to his, and kissed his mouth with a kiss so gentle, he surely must know what she meant. How much the thought of losing him had terrified her.

"I didn't think..." he started again, "this would be the way you'd take my clothes off."

On the snowiest day, the sun could make an appearance. In the worst of times, something could surprise you so much that laughter was the only response.

Summer felt her mouth curve into a smile. The dark, heavy weight inside lightened, dissolving like molasses in water. She rubbed his back as hard as she could without hurting him. "You're an idiot." There was no sting to her words, just warmth. "A crazy, brave, impulsive idiot. Don't ever do that to me again." She ran her hands over his broad shoulders, down his firm biceps and over his elbows. "I think you're warming up." She eased back a little to touch his chest. Yes, he definitely seemed less chilled. She wrapped her arms around him, and leaned close to press her entire body against his once more.

His eyes closed.

She slapped him gently on the cheek, and his eyes shot open again. "No going to sleep. It could be dangerous for you to sleep now. You need to warm up and get something hot into you—some tea or soup. How are you feeling?"

His lips had regained their natural color; all tinges of blue had disappeared. She ran a hand over his face, noting with approval the difference in temperature. The clamminess had gone, and it was no longer that horrible candle white.

His head moved a little forward, then back. "I'm feeling better." He still looked terrible, but at least he didn't look half dead any longer.

———

NICK WAS COLD—NOT frozen. Summer seemed to think he was incapable of feeling anything. When the opposite was true. She'd stripped off his clothes and rubbed him everywhere —absolutely everywhere—with the towel. Her heart was in the right place, but *Jesus*.

She'd thrown off her clothes, revealing her black bra and lace panties in front of him as though it was nothing. As though he was a block of ice.

He was as cold as one. But not staring at her body was difficult. In the same way as one shouldn't look a gift horse in the mouth, it was as impolite to look a gift girl in the boobs. Even if she was trying to save you from freezing to death. He'd never been happier to dive under a quilt, but then she'd climbed in after him and given him full body resuscitation.

The shivering had stopped. His skin felt cool, rather than frigid.

Apart from one, very hot area.

"I'm not apologizing for that." He looked down. "I don't have any control over it."

Her face went pink. "I understand."

"It's because you're not wearing much and you're wrapped around me like a vine," he said. "My body thinks it's Christmas."

"It almost is." She didn't attempt to move away. Her hand traced lazy circles on his back. "I think you're warming up nicely."

"I am." Heat permeated through him, like warm milk on a stove. "I feel much better." He angled around her to look at the dog in the basket. "He looks okay too."

"I dried him off, and he's so close to the stove I reckon he should be okay." Her hand kept moving, and her leg was still over his thigh. "What you did was very dangerous. What if I hadn't been able to pull you out?"

He nodded. He'd acted on instinct, rather than using his brain. The current was flowing so fast both of them could have been drowned. "I'm sorry I frightened you. I just couldn't—"

"Couldn't let Fella be washed away." She chewed her bottom lip. "I know. We both have become ridiculously attached to that dog. I hope he appreciates it."

"He must be feeling a lot better. He took off after that rabbit like a rocket. There's definitely a hint of collie in him."

She stroked his shoulders.

His cock jerked against her stomach.

She smelled of flowers, of lemon, of summer. Of Summer. He pushed back her cloud of tawny gold hair back from her face. Saw her eyes change as she stared up at him. "Thank you." He kissed her cheek.

Her chin tilted up, bringing her mouth into alignment with his.

This time, when they kissed, there was no trace of alcohol in either of their bodies. No clouded thinking. She made a small sound, somewhere between a sigh and a moan, and deepened the kiss, arching her back to snuggle in to him.

So far, she'd been the one touching. Rubbing. Holding. As the heat flooded through his body, warming the blood in his veins, Nick felt as though he'd been injected with a shot of adrenalin.

Her body was beautiful. He wrapped his arms

around her, and stroked down the long length of her spine, nape to base.

She shivered, but not from the cold.

His fingers traced the waist of her panties, then he slid his hands up her back again, and undid her bra.

She did a weird move, a sort of undulation and wriggle, and then the bra was off, and her naked breasts were against his chest.

"They're cold." He cupped both of them. "Gorgeous, but cold." He trailed his lips down her neck, tasting a trace of salt on her skin.

"I'm warming up too." Her voice was husky, low, aroused. "I wish this sofa wasn't so narrow." She stroked the side of his face. "Will we go upstairs?"

"To your bed?" This was getting out of control fast. The thought of spending the rest of the day in bed, exploring every inch of her with intense focus was difficult to resist.

"I want to have sex with you, Nick."

Have sex. *Condom.* "Do you have any condoms?" There was probably one in his wallet, but *one...*

"I..." She pulled a face. "No. I don't. I used to be on the pill, but..."

"I think I have one." He stroked his thumb

across her cheek. "Should we use it now or save it for later?"

She rubbed her eyes. "I don't believe this. One condom." She blew out a breath. "I wonder if Declan left any."

At the mention of her brother, Nick shook his head. "I doubt it. Those he would have taken with him to Andalucía. And if you suggest going and trying to find some in your parents' room..." He wrinkled his nose. "You'd get the same response as you did when you gave me your father's underwear."

"Oh boy." She eased away a little. "I vote we use it later."

"That's if I even have one in my wallet." There was a hidden pocket, which could be filled or could be empty.

"If not, we'll just have to be creative."

He loved this discussion.

NINE

Getting carried away in the heat of the moment was one thing—discussion about the finer points of contraception quite another. Summer couldn't pretend to herself that she hadn't thought through sex with Nick any longer. Couldn't blame drink, or circumstances. *Who's going to know?* She brushed off the anxiety clenching her stomach muscles tight. In Brookbridge everyone knew everybody else's business; you had as much chance of keeping a secret as you had winning the lotto. But up here, sequestered from the rest of humanity by the elements, with the nearest house a couple of miles away, their secret would be safe.

No-one need know. It didn't have to mean anything.

Still, the discussion has altered the mood from uninhibited to reserved. She still wanted him, but the desperate edge had been eroded from her desire. Maybe they should get on with the jobs for the day that needed to get done before nightfall. It would be dark by five or six, more than enough hours then to explore each other.

She climbed off the sofa and put her clothes back on. "You need to eat and drink something hot." She filled the saucepan and put it onto the woodstove. "And we should try to find out when the electricity will be restored."

"Summer..." He reached a hand out to her. "Come and sit down here for a moment." He patted the sofa.

She didn't want to. Didn't want to get drawn in. "No...I'll just...I'll make some coffee." She had no idea what she was getting herself into here, no idea at all. There was a pile of reasons they shouldn't do this, a pile as high as the Christmas presents that would be under her brother's Christmas tree. And only one reason they should. Because they wanted to. Desire. Nothing more than that. No love, no happy ever after. No even pretense of a relationship. It was damned depressing.

"We can wind back time to before I woke up this morning. Pretend all of that never happened."

He looked so serious her heart twisted. "Do you want to do that?"

He shook his head. "No. I want to take you to bed, and be creative. But you have reservations...I can see them in your eyes."

Summer cleared her throat. "It would just be sex." *Laying down ground rules.*

"No, it wouldn't."

And getting them stomped on.

"There's no way being with you would just be sex," he said. "We've known each other for years, we have a deeper connection, it would..."

"Be just sex."

His eyebrows pulled together. His forehead wrinkled. And his mouth turned down at the corners. "How could it be?"

"It would have to be—"

A loud buzz reverberated through the kitchen table. Then again. Nick grabbed his cell phone and stared at the screen. "It's Declan." He put the cell on the table and let it ring. "I can't talk to him now."

"If we do this, you can't tell him. Ever."

His eyes widened. The phone kept ringing. "I can't keep a secret like that from Declan. He's my oldest friend. Why would we need to hide it anyway? Okay, it would be a shock, but once Declan and our families get used to it..."

Get used to it? "Neither your family or mine

will understand that you and I had a quick fling." She brushed her hair back from her face. "They'll think it was sleazy. They'll judge us."

"Judge you, you mean, don't you?" His mouth compressed into a line.

"Yes, they'll judge me. Women always get judged. Men don't."

"So you want a quick fling. Just sex. Secret sex. You don't want anything else from me."

"I want your silence."

He shook his head. "People in my practice know that I'm here—know that there is someone here looking after the house for the holidays. I didn't reveal your name, but I won't ask everyone to lie for me. To lie for you. Did you really expect that you could come back to Brookbridge and no-one would know?"

She'd hoped to.

"I have to call Declan back." He stood and picked up the phone. "And I won't lie to him."

———

NICK PLACED THE CALL. His friend answered immediately. "How's it going? I guessed you were probably with a patient—maybe stuck on a hillside with a freezing sheep or something. The weather forecast says there's snow in Ireland."

"Yeah, feet of it." He glanced at Summer who stood in front of the range, twisting her hands together. "Wish I was there."

"I bet." Declan laughed. "I'm calling to get your brother's number. Matthew is still in London, isn't he?"

"Yes, for a while anyway. He and April are coming over for Christmas, but they won't be making the trip for a few days. Maybe even longer if this weather keeps up. What's the problem?"

Declan and Matthew weren't friends, he could see no reason that Declan wanted to contact his brother. "It's Summer," Declan said. "We can't get through to her cellphone, and our parents are worried. They called the restaurant, but there's no reply from them either. We thought maybe Matthew could track her down, make sure she's okay. "

"Okay, hang on a moment." He put the phone on mute. "Your parents are trying to find you. Your phone is dead."

Her face crumpled. "The singing..." She rubbed her eyes. "The battery must be flat. I can't..." She paced the room. "Maybe I can call them from your phone—no, Declan will recognize the number—"

"They want Matthew to go out to your house and check on you. You'll have to tell them where you are. And I'll have to tell Declan the truth."

She rolled her lips in. Then gave a brief nod. "Tell him. Then put me on to them."

"Declan." Nick internally cursed her for putting him into this situation. "Summer is fine. She's here."

"What?"

"I'm in your parents' house right now. And Summer is with me."

There was silence for a moment. Then Declan spoke. "You want to tell me what's going on, buddy?" There was an edge to his words, as if he suspected them of being in collusion. Which, of course, they were.

There was no alternative but to reveal everything. Well, almost everything. The events of a few moments earlier didn't need to be revealed. "I got a call yesterday morning about an injured dog. It was Summer. She's hiding out at your parents' house for the holidays, and a stray appeared...anyway, the details aren't important. I came out here and fixed the animal up, but he was too weak to transport, so I stayed the night here. It's been snowing all night, and now we're marooned. Uh, the power is off too."

"So you're snowbound with my sister." Declan didn't sound happy about it. "Where's her boyfriend? What about the restaurant—surely she needs to be there, it's the busiest time of the year."

"I don't know." He didn't know much about anything where Summer was concerned. Except for the fact that all she wanted from him was sex. "You'll have to ask her about that stuff yourself. I'll put her on." He held out the phone.

Summer took it. "Declan?" She rubbed the back of her neck. Sat on the edge of the sofa. "I...um...I'm here."

The water was boiling. Nick threw back the quilt and pulled on the set of dry clothes Summer had brought down when she fetched the towels. She probably wanted privacy, but she wasn't getting it. He had questions. Unanswered questions. And if she wouldn't tell him what was going on, he would have to learn the answers by whatever means he could.

"No, no, everything's fine." Her fingers were clenched so tight, they'd gone white. "The power is out, so I couldn't charge my phone. Michael's working, and I decided I wanted to...um..." She was a terrible liar.

"Don't put me on speakerphone—" She closed her eyes and gritted her teeth. "Hi, Mum. Hi, Dad. Yes, I'm in Ireland. I just decided on a whim to come home for a few days. Michael's been working so hard, and the restaurant...well, I have a very good chef who's standing in for me for the Christmas period. I was getting burned out, you know, and I thought some time alone would be good." Had she even realized she'd crossed her fingers?

"He's...he's coming out in a few days. We'll be together for Christmas. I won't be alone."

I can't listen to any more of this.

Nick took the water off the stove, made a cup of coffee, and strode out of the room. She was spinning lies, maybe now, or to him the previous night. Either the relationship with Michael was history, or they'd had a lovers' tiff, and he was on his way in the next few days. *Who the hell knows?*

The sympathy he'd felt for her broken relationship evaporated. He'd been a fool. A complete and utter idiot. Why would she lie to her parents? Why pretend everything was fine, unless she expected it to be?

The memory of her anger when she'd revealed what he'd considered to be the truth the night earlier burned through him. *That was real.* Because the alternative, that she had mislead him because she wanted to go to bed with him, was too horrible to contemplate.

He'd said their family would be okay with them having a relationship—no wonder she'd fought so hard against that particular idea if Michael was waiting in the wings for their big reconciliation. He crossed his arms and stared out the window in the sitting room. It was starting to rain, which meant the temperature was rising.

There was no way in hell he was staying here a moment longer than he had to. No way he was playing any more of Summer's games.

He walked back through the kitchen where she sat, still talking to her family, and out the back door.

———

IF THERE WAS anything worse than lying to her parents and brother, it was the look on Nick's face as he passed her on the way outside. He hadn't even looked in her direction, but his anger was evident. What did he expect? That she'd just tell them the truth and have them worried all through the holiday?

There wasn't anything they could do from such a distance, and telling the truth would have them worried—she wouldn't put it past her mother to insist on flying back to Ireland.

When he came back in, she'd explain.

She wanted to be with him, wanted to chase away the ghost of her relationship failure and replace it with a new memory, a warm memory of Nick's lovemaking, but the prospect of another relationship...she shivered. *I'm just getting over the last one.*

Declan spoke, wanting to talk to Nick.

"No, Nick's not here. He's gone outside," she said. "Shall I get him to call you back later?"

"Do that." Her brother's voice was warm. "Take care, sis."

Her parents said their goodbyes, then they were gone. She stood up and walked over to Fella. "How are you doing?"

He lifted his head and whined. She checked his coat—dry. And temperature—warm.

"I think it's time for you to have some breakfast." She looked out the window as she filled a couple of bowls. Nick was trudging back to the house.

He pushed open the door, shaking water from his hair. Then shoved his hands into the pockets in Declan's sweatpants. "All done?"

"Declan asked if you would call him back."

"I'll call him later." He strode over and picked up his cellphone. "First, I want to call the electricity company and find out if they have a crew on the way." He barely glanced at her. "The rain is turning the snow to slush. We should be able to get out of here this afternoon. I want to get Fella into the surgery, he looks well enough, but that swim could set off a secondary infection in his leg, and I may need to give him antibiotics. I can't do that here."

He called directory enquiries, and then the electricity company.

"Nick…" She wanted to turn the clock back. Wanted to make him understand her reasons for lying to her family. "I…"

He held up a hand. "Hello? We've lost electricity here. I'm sure you have crews out, and just want to find out when we might expect it to be restored." He gave their location, and listened to their reply. "Fine. Thanks." He didn't look happy. "They have crews out, but they won't get the power on out here until tomorrow at the earliest. I don't want to leave you here without electricity."

"I thought…" She'd thought they'd talk it out, but now, looking at his face, that idea was dying. He didn't look as though he wanted to hear anything she had to say. "I want to talk about what happened. About what I told my family."

"You don't need to justify anything to me." His voice was calm, but a storm was brewing in his eyes. "Like I said, the reaction I had to you was out of my control. It didn't mean anything. Forget about it."

How could she? "I didn't lie to you…"

"If you didn't lie to me, you lied to your family," he said. "I can't see any reason why you would do that, so I have to presume you spoke the truth to them. And if Michael is going to make an appearance in the next couple of days, I don't want to be collateral damage." He stood up. "You'll have to come back to town with me and camp out in my spare room until the power is restored. I suggest you pack up whatever you need, including anything from the fridge which will spoil if you leave it here, and I'll shovel a path down to the road."

Before she had a chance to say anything more, he pulled on his boots, put on his coat, and left.

For a while, she just sat there. Nick could say what had happened between them didn't mean anything. He could brush it off as if it was nothing, just as she'd tried to, before the phone call. But the truth was that she'd felt more in his arms than she had during all the years with Michael. She'd wanted him. And when he'd risked death for Fella, she'd been so worried her heart had clenched. Nick wasn't just anyone. He was special. But he didn't trust her, and she couldn't really blame him.

Staying here alone in the dark and cold held no appeal.

He might not like her very much, but maybe if she stayed with him, she could make amends, make things better between them.

From the storeroom, she took a large cardboard box, carried it to the fridge, and started to pack.

TEN

They made it down the mountain and drove into Brookbridge at four-twenty. The going was slow, but the Land Rover made steady progress and the closer they got to town the clearer the road became. The gritting lorries had been out, adding salt to the main roads, so once they got through the snow-covered lane to the house it was easier. Nick focused on driving, and Summer sat in the backseat, turning around and reassuring Fella as they drove.

It was good to not have to talk to her—what was there to say, anyway?

He couldn't have left her in a cold house alone, but the alternative wasn't great either. His apartment was small; it would be difficult to share it with her. But there was work—he spent long hours at the practice as it was, having a houseguest wouldn't change that.

"I'll drop you at my apartment and then take Fella in to the practice."

"Okay," she said in a quiet voice. "Thanks for taking me in."

He indicated, and pulled up outside his apartment building. "Fella will be okay in the car for a few minutes." He climbed out and took the box of groceries from the front seat.

Summer gathered her things, and followed him to the door.

"It's warm in here." She glanced around. For the first time, he saw his home through someone else's eyes. The place was functional. He hadn't bothered much with decoration, apart from some family photographs on the mantelpiece. He put the box down on the kitchen breakfast bar. He rarely brought the women he dated back here, they usually ended up in their houses, and he usually left at some stage during the night—his work consumed him, and he'd never found anyone he wanted to spend more than a few dates with.

"There's plenty of hot water." He walked into the spare bedroom. "This is your room. There are sheets and blankets in the cupboard next to the bathroom." He shoved his hands into his pockets. "I better go. If you need anything..."

"I'll find it." Her smile was difficult to resist. "Thanks again, Nick. For everything."

He took a step back. "I may be late, so don't wait up." He gestured to the rack of take-out menus next to the phone. "All these guys deliver. The Chinese is good." Keys hung on a hook next to the front door. He picked one up and handed it over. "Here's a spare key for you." He opened the door wide. "See you later."

Familiar cars were lined up in the parking lot— Sean's, Evie's, and two cars for the temporary vets. He had to carry Fella out of the car, but once down, the dog trotted along next to him easily enough.

"You're back!" Evie walked around the desk on seeing him. "And you've brought a friend." She patted Fella's head. "Hi, boy." She looked up. "This is the patient?"

"Yes, this is Fella." They went into a treatment room. "I don't suppose you could get me a coffee, could you? Is Sean around?"

"I'll tell him you're back." She disappeared.

Moments later the door opened. "So, what happened to you?" Sean looked him over. "You look like shit."

"Well, I've been living in a house without electricity, I haven't showered for a couple of days, and I took a swim in the river this morning, courtesy of this guy." He jerked a hand toward Fella.

"You were out at Declan's parents' house?" Sean eyed him. "Evie said a woman called."

"Summer." There was no point in lying any more. "It was Declan's sister, Summer. She was staying there alone."

Sean didn't know her, but he knew of her, everyone knew of Summer Costello. "Doesn't she live in London?"

"Normally. She decided to spend Christmas in their house. The power is still out—she's staying with me for the time being."

"Bummer." Sean crouched in front of Fella. "That's going to cramp your style. I know how you love your privacy." It wasn't that he loved his privacy, it was just that he hadn't found anyone he liked enough to share it with. "Is she still staying for the Christmas party?"

The party. "Damn, I'd forgotten. When is that?" He seemed to have lost all sense of the date.

"Tomorrow night," Sean said. "Everyone is looking forward to it."

The annual Christmas party was in the local Italian restaurant, *Buona Vita*, with dancing afterwards at their nightclub, *Arabellas*. Everyone brought a date—everyone except him, he hadn't had a chance to ask anyone yet.

"You should bring her," Sean said. "I mean, you can hardly leave her on her own. I'd quite like to meet this Summer, anyway. Didn't she leave to run her own restaurant in London? So she's not married?"

Evie came in with a cup of coffee. "Thanks, Evie. You can't know how much I appreciate it." He sipped the hot liquid. "She's not married."

"Who's not married?" Evie asked.

"Summer Costello." Sean gathered supplies. "I guess we better get this dog up on the table and clean out his wound if he's been swimming in the river."

"Swimming in the river? Wow, this dog lives dangerously." Evie's eyes widened.

"Nick's been swimming too." Sean laid out a long strip of paper towel on the examination table. "Give me a hand."

Together, they lifted Fella onto the table.

———

NICK HAD SAID he would be late, and not to wait up, but she didn't believe him. He would be exhausted after the day they'd had, and he must want to shower and change. She spent an hour in the bath, luxuriating in the hot water. After living without hot water and electricity she realized how she took them for granted. She changed her clothes, and put on a load of washing—her clothing and

Nick's, and the borrowed clothing Nick had been wearing when he dived into the river earlier.

When he came in, he'd be hungry. She had unpacked her groceries into his barren fridge, and set to making a casserole, using chicken pieces that she found in the freezer, and her stock of fresh vegetables. She turned the television on to keep her company while she worked, and opened a bottle of wine.

Things had got way out of hand while they were in the mountains. If Declan hadn't rung, they would be eating there together, going upstairs to the bedroom she'd slept in since childhood, getting creative, and finally using the sole condom in the house. She swallowed a mouthful of wine. *Thank goodness that hadn't happened.*

Her stomach hollowed out at the memory of his mouth, tracing down her neck.

It's not a good idea. The memory of his body, long and lean squashed up against hers made her clench her thighs together in a vain attempt to quench the sensations that tingled through her, turning her muscles lax. Her nipples pressed against her clean bra as she remembered his touch, his scent, his feel.

If only they didn't know each other, if their lives weren't so intertwined that it was impossible to detach after intimacy.

She stirred the casserole and shoved it into the oven.

———

NICK SHOWERED and shaved at the practice, and dressed in spare scrubs. He'd checked Fella's stitches, cleaned his wound and bandaged it, and set Fella on a course of antibiotics, just in case. He'd put the dog in one of the cages in the surgery, but had already decided to take him home later, he didn't need to be there, and they needed the room for any unexpected patients. He filled out a patient card, and charged medicine to his own account. No-one would be paying for Fella's care, and even if someone tried to claim him, there was no way he'd hand the dog over to the person who'd treated him so badly.

Mid-afternoon, he received a call from Declan. "Is Summer with you?"

"No. I'm at work. The weather improved enough for us to make it back to Brookbridge. The power is still out at your parents' house, so I brought Summer back with me—she's staying in my apartment."

"Good. I don't like the idea of her at the house alone. I didn't buy that story she was spinning for a moment. There's something up. This time last year, she was rushed off her feet with bookings for the restaurant—I don't understand how she can leave it during the busiest time of the year. There's something off with her explanation of why Michael isn't with her too. How is she? Is she depressed?"

Nick didn't like keeping things from his oldest friend, but it wasn't his place to reveal that Michael and Summer's relationship was over, if indeed it was. "She doesn't seem depressed. Tired, yes. But not depressed."

"Can you keep an eye on her until Michael arrives?"

How could he refuse? "Of course. She can stay with me."

"That's great, mate." Declan sounded happier. "Something is going on with her—I can't work it out from a distance, but I'm relieved that you're there in my place. You know Summer, she always wants people to think the best of her."

Does she? It struck Nick that he didn't know Summer at all if that was the case.

"I better let you get back to it." They said their goodbyes.

When the last of the evening's patients had been dealt with, he changed back into the borrowed clothes and turned to Sean. "You want to grab some dinner?"

"Sure." If Sean thought it was strange that he

wasn't rushing back to see his house-guest, he didn't say anything about it. "The Farmers?"

"Sounds great." The Farmers Arms in the middle of the village served great home-cooked food, and right now he couldn't think of anything better than a plate of steak and chips and a pint.

It was strange to be back in civilization. Disconcerting to hear the buzz of voices, when for the past couple of days the only voices he'd heard had been Summer's and Fella's. "I'll go back and take Fella home with me tonight. He won't get a home before Christmas."

"It could be difficult to find him a home anytime—you know what people are like, they want cute puppies." Sean gulped his pint. "Might you take him?"

"Maybe." With all that Fella had been through he couldn't stand the thought of him ending up in a pound. Sean was right, and Fella was a large dog with an unknown history—it was by no means certain that he'd fit into a family with kids. The easiest solution would be to give the dog a permanent home. He'd always avoided the possibility of owning a dog, but Fella could come in to work with him everyday. "I think I will."

"Good." Sean lifted his pint. "Here's to the new member of your family then."

"To Fella." Their food arrived.

"So what's the story with Summer Costello? You didn't know she was staying in her parents' house, did you?"

"No." Nick had no secrets from Sean. "No one did. She was hiding out."

Sean's forehead creased. "I thought she was all set up in London."

"She owns a restaurant, and is in a long-term relationship. At least, I think she does. I'm confused, to be honest. Last night she told me the relationship had been over for months, but today she told her family Michael was joining her here for Christmas. I don't know what to think." He attacked his steak with a vengeance.

"If she's hiding out, it seems to me that she's hiding something. Maybe something she's ashamed of. Would the failure of a relationship be such a big deal?"

Summer was a success; everyone said so. Maybe confessing the truth, that her relationship had failed, would seem impossible?

"It shouldn't be. I mean, what is she going to do —pretend forever?"

"Or maybe it's a temporary thing, they're on a break, and she hopes they'll get back together before she has to tell anyone," Sean said.

"If that's it, I don't know why she'd tell me different." The more he thought about it, the more likely it was that Summer was lying to her parents. That she didn't want them to know that she and Michael were over. She'd said she didn't want anything to spoil their holiday. And her parents would definitely be upset if they thought she was spending Christmas alone. "I guess I'll have to talk to her. But not tonight. Tonight I'm so tired, I just want to eat and go home and crash."

———

AFTER A NIGHT OF BROKEN SLEEP, Summer climbed out of bed and got dressed. She hadn't bothered to unpack. The repair crew had said they expected to get the electricity back on within twenty-four hours, and once that was done, she'd go back home. It was six days before Christmas, and the thought of the long, lonely days stretching out before her held little appeal.

But she had things to do. She'd brought her laptop and a file of accounts from the restaurant, which she wanted to get square before she returned to London. It had been hard to accept the failure of the business that she'd poured all her hopes, and her money, into. She should have given up earlier, but she'd soldiered on, pouring good money after bad until she was so cash-strapped that she'd been forced to let staff go.

At that stage, there was no chance of crawling her way back.

She'd put the restaurant up for sale as a going concern, and hoped to find a buyer soon. At least the bank was being reasonable—for the moment.

But the collapse of the restaurant meant she no longer had anywhere to live in London too. She'd spent the previous week in a hotel, and then had to face facts. There was nothing keeping her in London any longer. Her savings had been depleted to such an extent that with no job she couldn't afford to rent anywhere.

And long days and nights concentrating on the business meant she had acquaintances, but no friends—the friends she and Michael made together had been his friends before they moved in together, and remained his friends after they broke up.

Her best option was to return to Ireland, find a position as a head chef, and pay off the remainder of her debt from a distance.

Summer's idea was to formulate a repayment plan. Find somewhere cheap to live, or failing that, move back in with her parents, and to find a job locally. Moving home was humiliating, but might be her only alternative. The money she would save on rent would go toward clearing her debt. Her parents had invested in the restaurant. It would take years to pay them back, but not doing so wasn't an option.

Even though he had told her not to, she'd waited up for Nick the previous night—only giving up on him when her eyelids were drooping with fatigue. She'd turned off the oven, and crawled into bed. If he came in some time during the night, she hadn't heard him.

She pushed open the door of the bedroom and stepped out.

A bark. "Fella!" The dog trotted over and shoved his nose into her outstretched hand. His tail whipped back and forth in a frenzy of delighted welcome. She crouched, and rubbed the dog's head, crooning to him.

"Good morning." Nick stood in the kitchen, holding a mug. "You want some coffee?" He looked different this morning. Less angry.

"I sure do." She walked over, Fella at her side. "I thought he was staying in at the vets."

"There's no need. He doesn't need any more medical attention—what he needs is a home, to gain weight, to become acclimatized to people. We don't even know if he's ever met any children, and it's unlikely he'd fit into an average family. There are too many variables against him finding a home through normal channels." He shrugged. "If he goes into the pound, he'll end up on death row. I couldn't face that so I've adopted him." His mouth curved into a smile. "Darned dog snuck under my defenses."

Summer's heart felt as though it had swelled in her chest. She couldn't stop smiling. "That's brilliant." She rubbed Fella's ears. "I can't think of a better person for him to live with."

They'd brought the basket with them; it sat against the wall in the kitchen. "So I guess I'll have to beg another lift from you. Up the mountain. The repair crew is probably fixing the electricity today."

Nick leaned back against the counter. His gaze met hers and held. "Would you stay for a while longer? The practice are having their Christmas party tonight, I'd like you to come."

"You would?" She thought he wouldn't want anything to do with her after yesterday—he'd been so angry after overhearing the stupid lies she'd told her parents.

"Yeah, I would." He picked up his coat from the chair. "We need to talk. But right now, I have to go in to work. Can I leave Fella here with you?"

ELEVEN

The entire staff of Brookbridge Veterinary filled one huge table at *Buona Vita,* and all of them had dressed up for the occasion. Nick and Summer were last to arrive; heads swiveled at their entrance. After a quick introduction, they took their seats. Evie was sitting on Summer's right, and before long they were deep in conversation.

The small Italian restaurant was packed full; it had become a much-loved place to eat in the couple of years since it opened. The murmur of muted conversation and low lighting soothed away the cares of the day as Nick reviewed the menu and made his selection.

"Hi, Nick." He'd taken the waitress, Elaine, out a couple of times the previous summer. She was tall, slender and blonde—great fun, but they'd both realized fairly quickly that there wasn't enough of a spark between them, so they settled on being friends. "Long time no see." She rested a hand on his shoulder. "Have you decided?" She leaned over and pointed at the menu. "We've added a few things since you were last here. I know you love fish —the salmon ravioli is to die for."

"I'm divided between that and the beef medallions."

She shook her head, flirting for real now. "You need to get out of your comfort zone. You always have the beef. How about calamari deep fried, with tomato and garlic?"

"Take everyone else's order first, Elaine. I'll think on it."

She went around the table taking everyone's orders, then returned to him. "Okay, boss, what's it to be?" Her hand rested on his shoulder again.

"You sold me on the salmon." He grinned.

Sean had ordered wine for the table so he filled his glass then turned to Summer. "White or red?"

She was looking at Elaine, who was scribbling down his order. And she didn't look happy. "White, please."

He filled her glass.

She lowered her voice. "You must come here often, if the waitress knows your favorites."

"Elaine and I dated a couple of times."

"Nick has dated most of the women in Brookbridge," Evie teased. "Except me. My husband wouldn't approve."

"Oh yeah, he's a real heartbreaker," one of the vets, Alison, said. "I think I've only been safe because we work together." She leaned over to Summer. "Or maybe it's because I don't go for his type."

"Type?" Summer's voice sounded faint, as though she couldn't believe she'd fallen into the middle of this discussion.

"You're making it sound as though I'm a man-whore," Nick said. Sure, he'd dated most of the single women in Brookbridge, but he'd lived here forever. And there weren't that many of them anyway.

"What type is Nick, then?" Summer asked again, looking more than interested in Alison's answer.

"Male." Alison grinned. "I only date women."

"So you're not married?" Evie tilted her head to the side as she quizzed Summer. She always had to know everything about everyone—was obviously keen to rip away the veil of secrecy and find out what exactly Summer was doing in Brookbridge.

"No. I'm just out of a relationship."

The truth. Surprised, Nick gazed at her. She'd

worn her hair up in a twist and added long earrings that dangled almost to her shoulders. Her black dress was subtle, revealing the long column of her throat, the curve of her neck and dipping down to a hint of cleavage. Hardly seductress wear, especially compared to the short skirt and plunging neckline that Evie sported, but he found himself unable to look away. A beaded necklace sparkled at her throat. Her slender arms were bare. His fingertips tingled at the memory of how they felt to the touch. Soft, warm.

"You're staying with Nick?" Interest sparkled in Evie's eyes.

"For tonight, yes." Her gaze flickered up to his, then returned to Evie. "My house—my parents' house—has no power at the moment."

"You were lucky to be out of the office," Alison said. "We had Mrs. Malarky's poodle in again."

"Oh no. Not again." The dog had a penchant for chocolate, and on two previous occasions had arrived at the practice and had to have its stomach pumped. "The usual?"

Alison's nose wrinkled. "I caught that one. You owe me."

"Nick did great work with the dog I found in the woodshed." Summer took a sip of her wine. "If he hadn't come out, I think Fella might well have died. I can't believe the difference in him now compared to when I found him. He growled every time I came near, he wouldn't even let me touch him, but when Nick tried..."

"Aw, we don't call him the pet whisperer for nothing," Sean said.

"Fella ran off after a rabbit yesterday," Summer continued.

Oh no, she wasn't going to tell this story was she? "Summer..."

She glanced his direction. One eyebrow rose.

"I don't think everyone needs to know that story." His behavior had been reckless. He'd be teased about that escapade forever...would never hear the end of it...

"What story?" Evie's eyes rounded. "Tell!"

———

MOST PEOPLE at her end of the table had stopped talking when Evie spoke, but she wouldn't continue without Nick's agreement, so Summer waited.

Eventually, he shrugged and nodded.

"I've never seen an injured animal move so fast," she said. "But the moment a rabbit popped out of a hole, he was right on it. I ran back inside and..."

"Woke me up," Nick added, with a frown that made everyone laugh.

"Anyway, Nick took off after Fella, blowing a dog whistle."

"I knew that whistle would come in handy!" Alison leaned over the table to Summer. "He always carries it," she said in a stage whisper.

"I ran after them. The whistle caught Fella's attention when he was at the riverbank. He turned, then he lost his footing and slid on the frosty bank, and slipped into the water."

There was silence as everyone pictured the scene.

"The current was flowing really fast, and of course, the water was icy...then Nick stripped off his coat, pulled off his boots, and dived in after him."

"Jeez, that's crazy," Evie breathed.

"That's what I said."

"Huh, I don't remember you saying anything," Nick pulled a face. "You screamed and shouted to wake the dead though."

"I couldn't believe it, that's why." Summer shook her head, remembering. "I thought for a moment that was the end of both of you. I must admit I was wondering how on earth I'd explain having lost both the patient and the vet."

A ripple of laughter.

"I mean, can you imagine?"

"There would have been one hell of a call-out

charge involved if you'd had to make that call," Sean said.

"So, what happened next?" Evie was sitting on the edge of her seat.

"She wrapped her leg around a tree stump and pulled both of us out." Nick held up his glass of wine. "To my savior. To Summer, everyone."

Everyone lifted their glasses. "To Summer!"

"You must have been freezing," Evie said. "I bet it was straight home to a hot bath—no, hang on, there was no power..." A smile lifted the corners of her mouth. "How did you warm up?"

Oh crap! She should have seen that one coming. Summer felt her face heat, and knew she must be as red as the marinara sauce on her pasta.

"I had to strip in the kitchen and Summer shoved me under a quilt on the sofa." Nick smoothed over the next events with admirable aplomb. "Then it was hot tea, hot soup, hot water bottles..." *Hot loving.*

"Well, thank God you pulled him out," Sean said. "Life would be very boring without Nick Logan in the world."

"And you," Evie reached around behind Summer to swat Nick on the shoulder. "We all know you've got an overdeveloped protective instinct when it comes to creatures in trouble," to Summer, she confided, "he can't resist helping animals that need him, never could." Then she directed her attention to Nick again. "You need to put yourself first, boss. You matter too."

"Damn right." Sean thumped Nick on the back. "Now I understand why you're adopting Fella, you've got a lot invested in that dog."

Once the story was told, everyone started to talk amongst themselves. Summer sneaked a peek at Nick. "That wasn't so bad, was it?"

"Thanks to my quick thinking," he said in a whisper. "I thought I better rescue you when Evie asked how I got warmed up." He smiled, but there was heat in his eyes, passion banked. "I think we should keep that to ourselves."

"Oh, definitely." She compressed her lips to stop smiling.

"I want to talk you into staying with me for a while."

"You do?" She hadn't seen that coming. "I don't need to. Once the power's back on, the house will be very comfortable."

"Why be up there, alone, when you could be sharing air with me and Fella?" He leaned close enough so that no-one could overhear. "I'd like you to stay with me." Close up, she could see the darker flecks of green in his eyes. "Unless Michael is joining you."

She shook her head. "He isn't. I just said that...I

panicked." Confessing felt good, felt right. "I didn't want them to be worried—didn't want them to know it was over. I'll tell them in January."

"So you will be alone." Everyone was packed so tightly around the table, Nick's thigh brushed against hers. "I don't want you to be alone. You don't even have any decorations up. Or a tree. A house needs a tree."

"You don't have a tree either." She tried to not be so aware of him, but it was impossible. He was so close she could feel the heat radiating from his body. If she leaned sideways a little, her arm would brush against his...

"We could get one tomorrow." His smile would melt chocolate. It was certainly melting her. "Although bringing a tree into the apartment and persuading Fella not to pee on it might be a challenge."

She could say no. Stay up in her parents' house, worried about the future or she could accept his offer. It was a no-brainer. "Okay." She bit her bottom lip. "Let's do it."

———

EVERYTHING BETWEEN THEM HAD CHANGED. Nick felt schizophrenic—outer him was talking, laughing, sharing stories and paying attention to the chatter around the table, while inner him was focused on Summer. His ears were attuned to every sound that she made, every word, every laugh. When she brushed against him reaching for the wine bottle, a sizzle of sensation raced up his arm. He imagined he could pick out her scent above the aromas of Italian food. He tried not to look at her, but kept finding he was.

Because tonight she was coming home with him. In hours, they would be alone. And he didn't care if she wanted to keep secrets, wouldn't believe her if she said it was just sex again. He had time to change her mind. Had time to show her different.

She was talking—weaving Summer magic—and the people he worked with every day were captivated. She fitted into his life as easily as Cinderella's foot fitted into the glass slipper. She didn't want to tell him anything more about what was happening in her life—didn't want to talk about Michael or the restaurant, and the compulsion to know had evaporated like flaming brandy over a Christmas pudding.

He could wait.

She'd tell him when she wanted to.

When the meal was over, the group headed out of the restaurant, and in to the club next door.

"We won't stay long," Nick told Summer. He wanted nothing more than to take her home—for them to be alone. But the Christmas party was far from over yet, there'd be more drinking, some dancing, before they could call it a night.

"Are you a good dancer?" She grinned. "I don't remember ever seeing you dance before."

"In that case, you have probably never seen me dance. I've been told my moves are unforgettable."

"I'd believe that." Her voice was husky. She glanced at his mouth quickly, then looked away. "I've found your moves unforgettable so far."

He took her arm, and ushered her to their table. The meal had gone on for a couple of hours, and as it was Friday night, there were many people in the club already. The air was warm and stuffy, and the bass of the music thudded through his chest. Everywhere, couples were dancing.

The moment Evie reached the table, she threw down her bag. "Sean. Dance?" Before he had a chance to respond, she'd grabbed his hand and pulled him up to standing.

Sean was no better a dancer than Nick, but he gave it his best shot, waving his arms around doing a half-jog on the spot, a half-shimmy that was impossible not to smile at. *Better wait for a slow one.*

"Will we?" Summer's eyes held a trace of mischief.

"Let's have a drink first." He handed her the list of cocktails, and waved over a waitress. He'd parked his car at the rear of the restaurant, but had decided on his second glass of red wine, to leave it there overnight and take a cab home.

The waitress took their orders and brought them a couple of cocktails. A creamy concoction—brandy alexander—for her, and a martini for him.

"I really like the people you work with." She sipped her drink, leaving a trace of cream on her top lip that he wanted to lick off. "They're all very open and honest."

"Yes, they'll get more honest and open as the evening progresses. Last year, Susan told me all about her marriage problems." He winced. "In detail. Don't get me wrong, I'm happy to listen if I can help, but when it comes to discussing erectile dysfunction...well, I wish she hadn't shared. Luckily, she'd forgotten all about it by the next day."

Summer's mouth stretched in a grimace.

"And Sean told us all about the crush he had on Evie. The crush he spends the rest of the year pretending isn't there." He glanced over. The music had shifted to a slow number, and Evie was in Sean's arms. He probably didn't even realize he was stroking his hand down her back. Or that once again he was staring into her eyes as if she was the only woman in the world.

"Why?" Summer's forehead creased. "If he has a crush on her, why doesn't he ask her out? She obviously likes him." She stared at the couple slowly rotating on the dance floor. "Look at that smile. She looks as though she's died and gone to heaven."

"I don't know." He'd suggested to Sean more than once that he take Evie out on a date, but Sean had always brushed off the suggestion. Maybe it was because they only seemed to flirt when they'd both had a few drinks. He'd said he kept his distance because she worked for them, and it wouldn't be right to date a member of staff, but the real reason... "I think he worries that she might say no."

"That's crazy." Summer sipped her drink. "If he likes her, he should just go for it. I mean, you never know till you try, do you?"

"I guess." Watching them dance, so right for each other if only one of them would realize it and take it further brought his and Summer's situation into sharp focus. He too, had hidden his feelings—had spent years waiting on the sidelines for the right moment. And had been too late—she'd moved in with Michael.

He reached for her hand. "Let's dance."

TWELVE

They cut in through the crowd of dancers, first swirling around the periphery, then advancing in ever decreasing circles to the center of the dance floor.

The music was loud, too loud to talk easily, so Summer didn't even try, instead just enjoying the feel of his arms around her, his hand at the curve of her spine. Up close against him, she rested her head against his shoulder and breathed in his familiar scent.

The freedom of being taken at face value was exhilarating. None of Nick's friends cared if she'd had a relationship fail, none of them cared about the restaurant. They took her as she was—just Summer —conversation had been easy.

They had no expectations—and she didn't have expectations of them, so there'd been the opportunity to connect one to one, not have to share the things that made her spirits sink, or her gut to roil with worry.

They all had one thing in common—Nick.

And it seemed everyone had a story to share.

She smoothed her hand over his shoulder. His arm tightened in response, Peeking up, she caught his gaze and smiled.

He swirled her around as much as was possible in the tight confines of the space available.

The vet, Alison, had shared a story of the previous winter, when Nick and Sean had trekked out to a farm on the far side of Brookbridge, intent on digging out a number of sheep buried in the deep snow.

Evie told how he'd nursed a half dead chicken back to life after a particularly brutal moult—refusing to give up on the bird, the pet of a friend.

His colleagues admired and liked him. Not because of his achievements, because of who he was inside.

She wrapped her arms tighter around his waist, looked up at him. "Nick?"

He brought his face down close so he could hear. If she angled her head, her mouth could brush across his cheek. If he turned to her at the same moment, their mouths could meet. Warmth bloomed in her chest, spreading outwards.

"How long before we can leave?"

"Do you want to leave?" Awareness was in his eyes. "Are you not having a good time?"

"I'm having a great time." She gave in to the impulse to press her mouth against his jaw. "I...I just want to be alone with you."

He moved against her in time to the music, his hipbones pressing against hers. "If we rush off too soon, everyone will know exactly why we're leaving." His mouth curved in a smile. "I don't care if there's talk, but you might."

Right now, she couldn't care if everyone in Brookbridge knew she intended to spend the night in Nick Logan's arms.

He was hard against her. She pressed her chest into him, feeling her nipples tight inside the material of her bra. "I guess we should wait a while then."

"An hour should do it." He smoothed a hand down her back. "If we can wait that long."

"I guess kissing on the dance floor is out of the question." Her mood dipped.

His mouth tightened. "If I start to kiss you in full view of everyone, I won't stop." In the middle of the dance floor, surrounded by people, it was as if they were alone on an island. Marooned together in a sea of people. "And it would be just my luck for the music to change. I can't step away from you right now without scandalizing everyone." He rotated his hips to make his point.

"Maybe we could get some air?" She glanced to the door at the back of the club. As there was no smoking inside, a makeshift area had been set up outside, with outdoor heaters and shelter for the nicotine addicted.

"Good idea." He danced her to the edge of the dance floor, took her hand, and pushed open the door.

A couple of people sat on chairs, smoking. Nick tugged her to a secluded area at the periphery. The temperature was chilled, but the two large heaters cast out enough heat to stop them from freezing. And her internal temperature was boiling anyway. No-one even glanced in their direction.

"Here." Nick opened his jacket wide and she snuggled close. He wrapped it around her and brought his mouth to hers.

His kiss was tender—the way his tongue probed her mouth so perfect she couldn't hold back a sigh. His hands held her face, and something about the way he did that made her heart twist. He kissed her as though he'd wanted to do so for hours. As though it was the most natural thing to do in the world.

No-one had ever kissed her like that before, as

though kissing was as vital as breathing. When they pulled apart, her heart was racing and both of them were breathing heavily.

Nick rested his forehead against hers. "There's no way I can wait an hour."

She felt the same way. "We'll have to go back to the table, make our excuses."

"Give me a minute." He stepped out into the chill of the tiny yard, away from the heat of the burners. "Stay there. I'll think about being in the river instead of being in you; that should cool me down."

He walked across the tiny yard, examining the large planks that formed the back wall of the enclosure. Summer moved closer to the outside heaters, held her hands in a pretense of warming them. The other people there stubbed out their cigarette butts, and the sound of music filled the air as they opened the door to the club.

Nick turned, and walked to her. "Okay, we're good." He took her hand. "Let's make our excuses and get out of here."

———

DISADVANTAGES OF BEING A DOG OWNER? Having to put them out when you want to do something else entirely. The moment they entered the flat, Fella was there, limping toward them and wagging his tail. "I better put him out," Nick said.

"I'll just freshen up." With a shy smile, Summer walked off in the direction of the bathroom.

Nick opened the back door, and let the dog into the garden. His breath puffed out in white puffs of vapor in the cold air. The temperature was falling again and the threat of more snow was in the air. They should go back to Summer's parents' house in the morning, check that the electricity was back on. Gather up more of her things. She'd only intended to stay the night, but he'd promised Declan that she would stay with him until Michael arrived. And as Michael arriving was a fantasy, she would stay with him through Christmas.

He liked being alone—had never felt the need to invite someone to live with him, even short-term, but Summer was different. He liked having her around.

Fella limped back. "Okay, come on in." He checked that Fella had water. Then the dog settled down in the basket they'd brought from the house on the mountain. The basket that had now become Fella's. Nick turned off the light, closed the kitchen door, and went in search of Summer.

She wasn't in the sitting room— and the

bathroom door was open, with the light off. He pushed open the door to his bedroom.

She had changed, and was in his bed. The entire scene had domesticity written all over it. For a moment, his insides rioted at the thought, but then she spoke.

"I thought I could be coy, could wait for you in the sitting room, or I could be brazen and just climb in here. This is where I want to be, so I decided to just go for it." She chewed her bottom lip, and there was indecision in her eyes, nerves. As if he might have changed his mind in the moments standing outside, might have come to his senses.

No chance.

Nick stripped off his clothes. Then walked to the bed, pulled back the cover and slipped between the sheets. "Come here."

She scooted over. "What's this?" He examined the overlong tee-shirt she was wearing, her legs bare under it. A large picture of a skull and crossbones graced the front.

"A Christmas present from my brother last year." She shrugged. "He thinks I still have a thing for pirates."

The mention of her brother made him hesitate for a microsecond. There would be no going back from tonight. No way he could pretend that nothing had happened between him and his best friend's sister. They weren't kids any longer and Declan would have to accept that. He imagined himself in Declan's shoes, discovering that Declan and his sister Amy had slept together. He wouldn't be delighted about it, but he'd have to accept it. As long has Declan hadn't taken advantage of her, as long as it meant more than sex.

"Do you still have a thing for pirates?" He eased the tee-shirt up and off, ran his palms over her naked, perfect breasts.

She sighed. Her arms came up and her fingers speared through his hair. "Hell no. That fantasy has been blown out of the water by my vet fantasy."

He pressed his lips to hers. With a moan, she opened her mouth, allowing him access. His hands stroked her, teased her nipples, which had already peaked into hard nubs. *God, she's so beautiful.* Their legs tangled, her thigh over his, and her silk panties brushing against his cock.

The only sounds in the room were of their sighs, hitched breaths, moans. She pushed him back against the mattress, and straddled him, still somehow keeping their mouths fastened together. The freedom to touch her soft skin was exhilarating. Her breasts were within reach of his mouth, so he licked one erect nipple and surrounded it with the heat and wetness of his mouth, flicking his tongue over the nub. She responded like a woman overcome, clutching him to her, eyes wild.

When he transferred his attention to her other breast, she wriggled against him.

"I better put on a condom." He reached across to the bedside table, and retrieved the small foil packet. Ripped it open, and sheathed himself.

As he did so, she shimmied out of her tiny panties, and kicked them to the bottom of the bed. When she returned to him again, she pressed her core against his erection. "I want...I want you."

He wanted to be in her more than he'd ever wanted anything in his life, but the first time with Summer wouldn't be rushed—wouldn't be ordinary.

"Not yet," he whispered. Then he clamped his arms around her, and flipped their positions so she was flat on her back on the sheets next to him. "Not yet."

———

MUSSED BY HER HANDS, Nick's hair tumbled over his forehead. His face held such raw sexuality she couldn't look away. He stroked her face with his fingertips, tracing the bump of her eyebrows, the slide of her cheekbones.

"I like touching you." His voice was deep and serious. His fingertips skated over her lips, skied the slope of her throat, and circled the base, between her clavicles.

None were traditional erogenous zones—but his touch was all the more meaningful for that.

He flattened his large, warm hands over her, and felt her body, from her shoulders to her belly button. Not lingering, just transferring heat, stroking her as he might stroke a cat.

Entranced, she lay still and watched him.

He shifted his position, ran his palms over her thighs, and then gently hooked a hand behind each knee.

Her breathing hitched at the look in his eyes as he placed one leg and then the other over his shoulders, and brought his head down to the juncture of her thighs.

In three, long years, Michael had never paid her such focused attention. Had never made her pleasure his priority.

Nick rubbed his thumb over her clitoris, moving in slow circles that made delicious tension curl in her stomach. His mouth covered her, and his tongue flicked inside her heat. One hand smoothed over her lower stomach, holding her in place as he kissed, tasted, teased.

Summer closed her eyes and bit down on her lower lip. The sensations were amazing—colors swirled behind her eyelids, and heat flared through her body, travelling from his mouth to her stomach, her heart, her arms, and stealing the strength from her legs.

His fingers filled her, the melting feeling changed. Like a gathering storm, everything seemed to rush together, circling beneath her belly button, rushing down...a tsunami, impossible to control, inescapable...

"Come." Nick's soft-spoken plea dissolved the last vestige of resistance. Her toes pointed, the back of her calves pressed against the warm, strong muscles of his back, and Summer surrendered, feeling the pulsing contraction and relaxation of her inner muscles spasm into bliss.

Maybe he could tell—maybe he realized just how affected she had been by the experience—or maybe he was just a man in a million, because Nick seemed to know exactly what she needed in the aftermath of her orgasm. She needed to be held.

He scooted up and tumbled her into his arms, holding on tight and smoothing his hands down her back in a way that made her feel...made her feel loved.

Loved. Summer breathed in deep, and tried to quell the misty, soft feelings swirling inside. *This is crazy.* Nick didn't love her, and she didn't love him. *Where are these feelings coming from?*

He was hard against her stomach. Making no

attempt to do any more than comfort. The intimacy and lack of control over her reactions to him made her anxious. She reached up and stroked the side of his face. Then kissed him, hard, demanding, urgent.

Her other hand slid down his back and rested on his butt.

Nick groaned.

Summer wriggled her hips, eased her legs apart a little, and squeezed. He read her body language perfectly, positioning himself at her entrance, and entering her in one swift thrust. As they rocked together, she forced down the thought that this was perfect, that this was where she was supposed to be, that Nick was the one.

Her foot linked around his calf, holding him in place as he thrust into her. She didn't think she could come again so hard, so absolutely, but he proved her wrong. And when she scaled the peak and soared over the other side, he was right there, with her, sharing the moment—sharing heaven.

THIRTEEN

Whoever wrote that women liked to snuggle, was guilty of one hell of a generalization.

Summer couldn't get away quick enough. After the best sexual experience of his life, his partner in lust shimmied to the edge of the bed, made some flimsy excuse, and followed it with a sprint to the bathroom.

Nick lay there, staring after her. *What just happened?* He wasn't arrogant, but there was no way what they had just shared was anything other than spectacular, for both of them. The noises she'd made, the way she'd clutched around him, her inner tremors and the marks she'd left on his back were all sure indicators that she'd been as affected as he was.

So why the midnight sprint?

The urge to climb out of bed and join her in the shower that he could now hear running behind the bathroom door, was strong. But he shut down the compulsion. Something was up. He had no idea what was going on with her, but she needed time for some reason.

After ten minutes, the bathroom door opened, and Summer appeared, wrapped in his navy bathrobe. It was so big; it covered every inch of her. She'd rolled up the arms, and tightly knotted the belt at the waist. Her hair was wrapped in a towel.

"I'm going to make some tea." She smiled, but put the toes of one foot on top of the other. "Do you want some?"

Nick shook his head. "I'm too tired. Bring it back to bed?"

She swallowed. "I...I'm going to dry my hair in my bedroom after. Um...I think I might just stay up for a while. I have problems sleeping. I don't want to disturb you with my tossing and turning all night." The look on her face, as if she expected a fight about her decision, gave him pause. He knew that look—he'd seen it on his own face often enough. It was the I-don't-want-you-getting-attached look.

He should feel happy that she didn't want any more than sex from him—he certainly wasn't interested in a relationship, but her making the decision rather than him nudged him off kilter.

He wanted her to stay. There was nothing he wanted more than to curl around her and drop off to sleep, but it wasn't as big a deal as she seemed to think it was. If she didn't want to spend the night with him, there was no point in making her feel bad about it.

"Okay." He put his hands behind his head. "If you change your mind, I'll be here."

"Great." With a smile, she headed for the door. "If I don't see you before tomorrow, sleep well."

She hurried from the room, and he heard the door open to the spare bedroom soon after, and the sound of her hairdryer.

It was ridiculous to feel bereft at her absence— he'd often slept with someone then headed back home afterwards, leaving them happy and satisfied. Or so he'd thought. Maybe when emotions were involved it wasn't as simple as that?

———

SUMMER WAS beyond relieved that Nick hadn't questioned her and had accepted her decision to spend the night in the spare room. After making love with him, she didn't think she could take any more intimacy. In the club, she'd been so desperate for him, so determined that tonight should end up with them together, that she hadn't taken the time to consider the consequences. She'd been expecting sex, not lovemaking, and the difference had never seemed so stark.

How could she keep things simple, when he affected her so strongly that she felt as though his arms were home?

Maybe it was because she'd known him forever, but casual sex with Nick Logan wasn't possible, she knew that now. She'd needed to regroup, to get herself together. And she'd be forever grateful that he hadn't made a big deal out of it, as Michael would have.

Despite her assertion that she'd suffer from insomnia, by the time she'd finished her tea, her eyelids were drooping, and her body was languid and sleepy. She'd climbed the stairs, and walked past his bedroom door, into the small spare bedroom. Lying in bed, she'd listened out for sounds of him, but the house was quiet, so she'd closed her eyes, and in moments, had fallen into a deep dreamless sleep.

A tap on the door woke her. Nick pushed the door open. "I brought you some coffee." He walked over to the bed. "Breakfast is almost ready."

She sniffed. "Are you cooking bacon?" She sat

up in bed and took the coffee from his outstretched hand.

"Bacon sandwiches." He made no move to kiss her, which perversely left her wishing he would.

"I'll be down in a couple of minutes."

With a nod, Nick turned and left the room.

It was as though last night hadn't happened. As if she'd dreamed it. *But I didn't*. Summer clambered out of bed, and dressed quickly. She washed her face in the bathroom, brushed her teeth, and tidied her hair, then went to find him.

He was standing at the oven, plating up the cooked bacon.

"I didn't even say good morning." She crossed the room and stood next to him. Close enough to touch.

He turned.

She curled her fingers around his upper arm and went up on tiptoe to reach his mouth. "Good morning," she whispered against his lips, then she kissed him.

"Good morning to you too." He snaked an arm around her and pulled her close, matching her gentle kiss and raising it to deep and sexy. When he let her go, her heart was pounding. *So much for dialing down on the love stuff...*

He picked up the plate of bacon and placed it on the kitchen table. "Breakfast."

"So what's on the agenda for today?" She felt light and happy, ready for anything. "Did you say something about a tree?"

"I don't normally bother, but..." he shrugged, "I guess if I'm having a guest for Christmas, I should make an effort. You are going to stay over Christmas, aren't you?"

The idea of spending Christmas alone in her parents' house held no appeal. "I'd like that." She paused. "But you have to cook dinner for your family, don't you?" She glanced around at the tight confines of the kitchen. "Is that here?"

"No. At my parents' house." He grinned. "You'll have to come with me."

"Well, if I'm spending Christmas with you, I'll have to help you out with your dinner-making challenge."

Nick punched the air. "Yes! I'm saved."

"Have you thought out the menu?"

Nick laid a couple of slices of bacon onto white bread and covered them in brown sauce. "Not really, as I said, I've booked a turkey—"

"One turkey does not a Christmas make." She tried to look serious, but gave up after a couple of seconds. "We need a plan." She looked around the kitchen. "Get me some paper and a pen and we'll write a list."

———

WHEN SUMMER HAD DRAWN up a comprehensive list of ingredients, including items he wouldn't have thought of in a thousand years, she subdivided the list into things to buy now and things to be delivered closer to Christmas.

"We can use internet shopping to organize a delivery to your parents' house," she said. "That means we don't need to worry about it." She waved the list in the air. "These other things we can buy today and cook beforehand."

Nick had an internet shopping account with the local supermarket. "We can do that tonight. We should head out soon, I want to drive over and check your house then we can get the tree and buy these other ingredients. I guess I should do some Christmas shopping too. I'm going to give Fella a bath today."

They sold collars and leads at the vets and he'd picked one of each up the day before for Fella. When breakfast was over Summer went back upstairs to get her coat and boots, and Nick fastened the red tartan collar he'd chosen around Fella's neck.

It had only been a few days, but already the dog was looking so much healthier. He seemed happier too—pressing his nose into Nick's hands and gratefully accepting a pat. It would be hard to manhandle him into the bath later, but well worth it.

"Ready to go?" Summer stood in the doorway bundled up in her coat, woolly hat, and gloves. He smiled at the memory of her sitting in bed playing imaginary drums with that hat on her head.

"Yes." They climbed into the Land Rover and drove up the mountain to the house. The salted road was clear, but snow remained on the verges, and the sky was pale blue without a cloud in sight. When they arrived at the house Nick checked the electricity was on and that the heating was working, while Summer packed the rest of her belongings and loaded them into her rental car. There was no point leaving it here, so she'd drive it back to Nick's house.

"When are your parents due back from Spain?"

"The third of January. I'd planned on returning to London by then, but they persuaded me to stay longer so we could catch up." Her nose wrinkled. "I guess I have some explaining to do."

"They won't be disappointed that you split with Michael, you know. I don't think either of them were particularly impressed with him."

She tilted her head to one side. "What do you mean? Did they say something?"

"No—I guess I'm mostly talking for your brother. He thought Michael was a bit of a dick."

Summer smiled. "Declan was one hundred percent right. I guess I just don't like having to admit that I made such a bad choice. I really thought he'd be there for me, but I couldn't have been more wrong. It makes me question how capable I am to make any decision, to be honest."

She was unnecessarily hard on herself. "Everyone makes a mistake sometimes—no-one's perfect," Nick said. "You're more perfect than most, but..."

She frowned. "What do you mean, I'm more perfect than most?" She crossed her arms. "I'm just the same as anyone else."

"No you're not." She'd never been ordinary, never been held to the same standards as everyone else. "You were always the best at everything, Summer. The best at school, the winner of everything, the girl voted most likely to succeed. Your parents are proud of you, and you've worked hard to live up to everyone's expectations, but you're not superhuman. You can fail. It's not the end of the world."

Her back was straight, and her shoulders had raised. She looked as though she was ready to fight a battle. "You make me sound like a robot." She glared at him. "I don't think I'm superhuman, I know I can fail."

This wasn't going the way he'd hoped, but there was no backing down on the truth now. "I don't think you do. If you did, you'd have told them your relationship is over. You wouldn't need to prove anything to anyone."

"You know what, Nick? Maybe we should just stop talking about me." She put on her coat and picked up her suitcase. "I don't have to justify my behavior to you, or to anyone else. I made a decision not to tell my family because I didn't want to worry them. I'm going to tell them in January. I don't want, or need your approval." She eyed him. "Maybe staying with you isn't such a good idea."

"I promised your brother I wouldn't leave you here alone." Nick crossed his arms.

Her eyes widened. "You promised Declan..." Her hands clenched into fists. "So all this time—you asked me to stay because Declan asked you to? Did he ask you to sleep with me too?"

"Summer..." *Shit, shit, shit.*

"Because you can tell my little brother I don't need to be babysat. I don't need..." Her eyes glistened with unshed tears.

In a couple of steps he was in front of her, hauling her into his arms. "I didn't ask you to stay because of anything Declan said." He stared into her eyes. "I wanted you from the first moment I saw you again, I want you for me, not because it's right, not because I don't think you can manage perfectly well without me, but for me. I want you, I can't help it. I don't want you to stay here, and I don't want you to leave in January and go back to London." Before he totally freaked her out and told her he didn't want her to ever leave, that he feared he'd lost his heart to her forever, Nick wrapped his arms around her and kissed her until he couldn't see straight.

FOURTEEN

Things were different between them as they walked around Brookbridge, doing their errands. She hadn't liked hearing his words back at the house—the plainly spoken assertion that she was afraid to be seen as anything less than perfect had stung—but Summer couldn't deny he was right.

There had been months to tell her family that she and Michael were over, months to explain that the restaurant had fallen into difficulty, and she hadn't revealed the truth. Mostly because she didn't want them to feel differently about her. To be disappointed.

Nick's words had been brutally honest. As had his declaration afterwards that he wanted her to stay not because her brother had asked him to, but because he wanted to. Wanted her.

With the supermarket shopping done, they loaded the bags into the Land Rover, and set out to buy a tree from the vendors set up around the supermarket car park.

"How about this one?" Nick strode right up to a tree that would fill the entire apartment.

"Too big." She pointed at a smaller one. "This one is good."

He examined the branches, the shape, and chatted with the vendor about the variety. She tugged Fella's lead when he wanted to go closer and sniff the tree. It didn't need watering.

"That's my dog." A hulking man stepped toward her, his gaze flickering from her face to Fella. "You stole my dog."

Fella stood so close it was as if he was stuck to her leg. His tail was between his legs. A low growl issued from his throat.

"Give me my dog back, right now." The man had close-cropped hair and wore a battered leather jacket and jeans. His eyes were a fraction too close together, and his yellowing teeth formed a snarl as he made his demand.

"This is not your dog." She held on tight to Fella's lead.

"He's my guard dog. You stole him." The man stepped so close she could smell his fetid breath.

"What's the problem here?" Nick slid an arm around her shoulders.

"Your girlfriend here has stolen my fecking dog."

"This is my dog." Nick stepped up, eye to eye with the stranger. "I found him half-starved a few days ago, with a gash on his leg."

"He must have got lost." The stranger's smile didn't soften his expression any. "No harm done. Thanks for looking after him. I'll take him now." He reached for the lead, but Summer pulled it back out of reach.

"No damn way." Nick put out an arm, and Summer and Fella sheltered behind him. "I'm a vet. What's your name?"

Summer took her cell-phone out of her pocket and snapped a picture of the stranger without him noticing.

"Why the hell do you want to know my name?" The stranger's hands curled into fists.

"Because I want to report you to the police for mistreating an animal," Nick said. "It's an offence, and you deserve to go to jail for what you've done to this dog." The anger in his voice made the stranger hesitate. "Come on, what's your name?"

"Listen, mate." The stranger took a step back. "Fine. If you want him, you have him. He's a useless mutt anyway." His leg jerked out in Fella's direction, in a kick that he'd probably delivered more than once, but he was too late, Fella skittered out of reach.

"Try that again, and I'll knock you out." Nick growled. He seemed bigger, more threatening than she'd ever seen him. "Piss off before I call the guards."

Without a word, the heavy-set stranger turned and disappeared into the crowd.

Adrenaline coursed through Summer's system. She crouched and patted Fella, reassuring him with words and deeds that he was safe, that he'd never see his awful previous owner again.

"Are you okay?"

She looked up at Nick, then stood. "You were bloody wonderful." She threw her arms around him and hugged him tight. "That man was a monster." She gazed out into the sea of people, but couldn't see him any longer. "You told him you were a vet— you don't think he'll try to snatch Fella do you?"

"I'd like to see him try." Nick's jawline was clenched tight. "I wish I knew who he was, I'd have him prosecuted. If he knows what's good for him, he'll stay away. I think he only tried it on because he didn't realize we were together."

He was right. If she'd been alone, maybe the

man would have just taken the lead from her and dragged Fella away. She shuddered at the thought. "I took a picture of him with my phone."

"Good. I'll take it to the local police. If he has any more animals I'll get the ISPCA involved, and they can stage a rescue." He looked down into her face. "Let's get our tree and go home."

———

SHE FOLLOWED him home in the rental car; together they brought the tree into the apartment and set it up on a stand by the window.

"Okay, where did you put those decorations we bought at the store?"

It was late afternoon and the sky was darkening. Summer walked to the drapes and pulled them closed. "In the kitchen, but I reckon we can trim the tree later." She turned. "I have something more urgent to do."

The look in her eyes... "What's that?"

Her fingers went to the front of her shirt and she started to unfasten the buttons.

"I want to go upstairs."

He didn't move. Waited for her to continue.

"I want to go to bed with you." She unfastened the last button, and her shirt fell open, revealing her hot-pink bra. "I want your hands on me." In two steps she was in front of him. "You were a hero today. Fella's hero. And mine too." She touched his face, traced his lips with her fingers.

She didn't need to say any more. Nick clasped her hand and together they walked upstairs.

This time, there was no slow, careful exploration of each other's bodies. They stripped off their clothes and, kissing, made it to the bed, all hungry mouths, tangled limbs and desperation. She cried out when he entered her. Wrapped her arms and legs around him so tight not a hair could come between them. They climbed toward the pinnacle in perfect synch, and came at the exact same moment, staring into each other's eyes, holding nothing back.

This time, she didn't climb out of bed after. Didn't try to deny what had happened. She snaked an arm around his waist, rested her head on his chest, and closed her eyes.

He stroked over her shoulder, down the soft skin of her arm. Breathed in the scent of her hair and her warm body. His body was languid, relaxed in the aftermath of their passion. *Perfect*. In moments, he was asleep.

Over the next three days, it was as though they'd moved into a different country, a country where they were the only inhabitants. There was no need to leave for supplies, no need to dress, no need to communicate with the outside world.

Time held no meaning; they ate when they were hungry, made love upstairs in bed and downstairs on the sheepskin rug before the fire, or on the sofa. Played chess, talked long into the night, about the choices they had made in their lives, the good times, the bad. Without discussing it, both had turned off their cellphones, not interested in what might be going on in the rest of the world.

There was no snow on the ground, but they acted as though they were snowbound—hidden from the rest of the world.

They were in bed mid-morning on the fourth day, when the doorbell's ring set Fella into a flurry of excited barking.

Summer sighed. "I guess we couldn't hide out forever."

Nick kissed her quickly, climbed out of bed and dressed. "I'll try to get rid of whoever it is. Stay right there." They'd made love late into the night, but he could think of nothing better than spending yet another day in bed. She sat up, her glorious hair tumbling over her shoulders, the curves of her breasts barely hidden by the silky, scarlet nightgown. Just the sight of her was enough to make him consider ignoring the doorbell.

Until someone stabbed it again, and Fella howled.

"Dammit." He shoved a hand through his hair.

Summer grinned. "I think I'll get up." She swung back the covers. "I could do with some coffee anyway." He frowned. She laughed. "Aw, come on, don't pout."

Nick took the stairs two at a time. Jerked the front door open, ready to give the visitor hell for their relentless doorbell-stabbing.

"Nick!" His sister, Amy, dived into his arms, and hugged him tight.

———

THE FRONT DOOR CLOSED, but the sound of voices still filtered upstairs. The mysterious visitor was here for a while.

Summer put on her shoes, and went into the bathroom.

I look different. The chronic case of bedhead was easily cured by the determined attentions of her hairbrush, but the other changes were more profound. Free from the pressure of the previous months, the edges of her mouth had lost their pinched look. She'd been so used to seeing the little wrinkle between her eyebrows, its absence made her trace her forehead with the tip of her index finger. The reflection staring back at her looked younger, freer, healthier, happier than she had in years.

She braided her hair, washed her face, and brushed her teeth.

Her makeup bag, on the bottom glass shelf to the side of the sink, hadn't been opened in days—she hadn't needed the armor of makeup alone with Nick—after a moment's hesitation, she unzipped it and took out a tube of foundation.

A few minutes later, she followed the voices into the kitchen.

"There you are. Coffee?" Nick stood up from the table as she entered. "I don't know if you remember my little sister, Amy." He couldn't have told Amy that there was anyone else in the house, because she was staring as though Summer was a mirage.

Nick tapped her on the shoulder. "Amy."

Her gaze flicked to him, whiplash style.

"This is Summer. Say Hi."

Amy swallowed. "Hi. Summer...that's an unusual name..." And then she got it. "Summer Costello? Declan's sister?"

"That's me."

Amy was out of the chair and across the room to Summer in a split second. "I don't think I've ever met you before—although of course, I've heard all about you from Declan over the years." She spoke so quickly she barely stopped to catch her breath. "I didn't know you were here. Are you staying with Nick?" Before Summer had a chance to answer, she was talking again. "We've been trying to contact him for ages, but his cell phone..." Her eyes widened. "Oh."

"Summer is staying with me over Christmas." Nick placed a mug of steaming coffee and a small empty plate in front of Summer, and pushed a white, cardboard box of pastries in her direction. "Amy brought cakes. What'll you have?"

"Umm." Summer selected an éclair and grinned at Amy. "Thanks, Amy."

Amy looked as though she was stuffed to the gills with questions that desperately needed answering. She rolled her lips together, and rubbed one hand over the other. Summer had no doubt that if she was alone with her brother there would be an epic inquisition taking place right now, but luckily Amy had been brought up right.

Interrogating just wasn't good manners.

"Amy's home for the holidays." Nick sat back down.

"Everyone's home for the holidays," Amy said. "And our mother is stressing out. She sent me to find out if you've changed your mind about cooking."

"Everything's under control." Nick picked up his cell phone and turned it on. "Oh, wow. I see what you mean. It looks as though she's been calling on the hour every hour." He tapped on the screen and put the cell phone up to his ear. "Mum? It's Nick. Sorry, I had my phone off."

The sound of his mother's voice was audible, the tone, but not the content.

Nick grimaced. "Okay, cool down. Yes, I'm ready. The supermarket is due to make a delivery to your house this afternoon." He rolled his eyes. "Yes, I'll be over tomorrow to start cooking. I'm bringing a friend to help me out."

He listened for a moment. "Summer Costello. She'll be joining us for Christmas...Uh huh... yes... restaurant in London." His gaze connected with Summer's and his eyebrows rose at whatever his mother was saying. "Oh, I didn't know her restaurant had a Michelin star. Lucky us, huh?"

Earning the Michelin star had been one of the high points of her professional career, but not even that had been enough to guarantee the restaurant's future. Dejected, Summer bit into the éclair, squirting cream out the side.

She walked to the cutlery drawer, and picked out a fork.

"Yes, we'll be there for dinner tonight, and I'll talk you through the menu then. What time are

Matthew and April getting in? Do you need me to pick them up at the airport?" Silence for a moment. "Okay, then. See you later."

He terminated the call, and checked his other messages.

"I said I'd do the airport run," Amy said.

"I know. Do you want me to take that off your hands? Mum said you're busy." Nick rubbed the back of his neck. "I've got a message here from the practice. I better call them back."

"I'd appreciate you picking them up." Amy stood up and put on her coat. "I'm gonna go." She pulled out a piece of paper from her pocket. "You were just the first item on my list, I've still a lot of things to do." She ran her finger down the list. "Where the heck will I get mistletoe?"

FIFTEEN

When the human whirlwind that was Amy had moved on, Summer went back upstairs to find her own cell phone. When she turned it on a flurry of messages landed.

Declan. Her mother. *What?* Six messages from Michael.

She sat on the bed and breathed in. *Why the hell is he calling?* Since they'd split she hadn't heard a word from him. For the first couple of weeks, she'd been so stunned, so upset, that she might have forgiven him if he'd told her it was all a terrible mistake, that he was sorry. But as time had stretched without a word—she'd faced the fact that she was alone. That she'd wasted three years on a man who was all style, no substance.

She didn't want to call.

She didn't want to have anything more to do with him.

She gazed at the last message, sent that morning. "Call me! Please."

Summer turned off her phone. Even if Michael prostrated himself on the ground before her, she couldn't see her way to ever going back into that relationship. She'd thought he was proud of her achievements, but now she saw things differently.

He'd like the kudos of being with a successful businesswoman. She'd hosted and cooked more dinners for his clients than she could count, and he'd shown her off as a trophy girlfriend. But when things became difficult, when she faced financial difficulties and struggled to make sense of what she needed to do to turn things around, he wasn't interested.

She'd spent night after night, listening to his work problems—had done her best to always bolster him when he was down, but hadn't received the same support in return.

She hadn't wanted to accept the truth that their relationship had been little more than an empty shell for the last year they'd been together. Accepting—admitting it to herself—meant that she'd failed. And even now, she'd lied to her family.

Being with Nick was so different. He accepted her for what she was, didn't care about all of that surface stuff. He liked her for her. She'd never been so caught up in anyone before, never felt so attracted, so...

In love. The words sounded in her head. Could she really be in love with Nick Logan? They'd never talked about what would happen when the holidays were over. He expected her to return to London, to a life that she didn't have anymore. If she was in Brookbridge permanently, would their relationship survive?

———

DUBLIN AIRPORT AT CHRISTMAS. A cross between a theme park and a zoo. Huge polystyrene polar bears and grinning snowmen posed in front of the floor length glass doors and windows, and harried travellers filled the rest of the available space.

The call into the practice had been to dole out Christmas presents...and afterward Nick hadn't been able to make as quick a getaway as he'd wished. So he was late.

He checked the arrivals screen, hoping they'd been delayed.

Landed. Ten minutes ago. With luggage to pick up, they wouldn't have made it out yet, so he jogged to the arrivals area, weaving through passengers and avoiding suitcases. He didn't know what made him turn, that particular moment. Maybe it was the way his body had twisted to avoid slamming into a woman charging through the crowd like an ocean liner.

He avoided the woman, but felt a slam in his heart the moment he saw the familiar face of the polished man in the impeccable black suit heading into the restroom. He'd only seen Michael once, but there was no mistake. Summer's boyfriend was in the airport. Carrying a suitcase.

For a moment, he just stood there, shock twisting his gut. She couldn't have lied—she wouldn't have...

There was one way to find out. He could follow Michael into the restroom and talk to him. Tell him...Tell him what? That he had fallen in love with Michael's girlfriend, that it was too late, he should turn right around and get on the next plane out?

She told her parents Michael was coming.

Nick gritted his teeth. His hands curled into fists. Summer was joining him and his family for Christmas dinner in two days; if there was another plan on the table she'd have to tell him before then.

He dragged in a breath, turned away, and continued running to the arrivals gate.

He was in place when Matthew and April, pushing a trolley laden with suitcases, came through a few minutes later. He waved to catch their attention, and walked to the end of the barrier to greet them.

"I thought Amy was coming!" Matthew enveloped him in a hug. "I guess you drew the short straw, huh?"

"Hi, Nick!"

He hugged his sister-in-law close. "I don't know about the short straw, Amy had a list as long as Santa's—I reckon I got off easy." He jerked his head in the direction of the exit.

They didn't seem to notice that he was quiet on the drive back to Brookbridge. Summer had said she had some errands to run—had she planned to pick up a certain someone at the airport too?

He wanted to drop and run, but the moment the car pulled up, his mother was out the front door waiting to hug the air out of everyone. "Help bring their things in, Nick. I've the kettle on."

He did as he was told. Greeted his father, whose features lightened in relief when he realized reinforcements had arrived. Christmas in the Logan household was a flurry of activity that started mid-November.

"We've been trying to get hold of you for days." He grabbed Nick's arm and pulled him to one side. "Are you really on top of the meal? Because if you aren't, tell me now before it's too late." He ran his hand through his greying hair. "I don't know why your mother made that stupid bet—she can't delegate *and* keep her blood pressure low."

"It's done. It's fine. There's a delivery arriving this afternoon."

"She said something about you having a chef to help out?"

"Summer Costello. Declan's sister. She's staying with me at the moment. She'll help me with everything."

Dermot Logan looked impressed. "I remember her. Fine girl." His shrewd look saw right through Nick. "You always had a thing about that girl."

He had. He did. And there was no point in denying it. "Yes. I always liked her."

"So? Is there romance in the air?"

A couple of hours ago he'd known the answer to that question. But now? "I don't know, Dad. Do me a favor, play the whole thing down with Mum, will you?"

———

FELLA STOOD up and trotted into the hall a minute before the front door opened.

"I'm in here!" Summer clicked the plastic top onto the container she'd just filled with her special cranberry and orange sauce.

Nick strode in. "Sorry I'm so late—there's no such thing as a quick cup of tea at my parents' house."

She walked over and hugged him. Just because she could. "What time do we have to be there?"

"We have about an hour." He puffed out a breath. "I'm exhausted."

"So, is everyone there?"

"More or less. My brother Finn and his wife live in Dublin so they'll be there. But my brother who lives in New York isn't coming after all— blaming the pressure of work." He rubbed the back of his neck. "So of course, there was much discussion about staging an intervention. It's not as though Adam is a drinker or a druggie, he's just in love with the wrong woman." He scowled. "I don't know why Mum and Amy think they have to go and get involved. They should just leave the poor sucker alone."

His relaxed mood of earlier seemed to have evaporated. "Why don't you have a nap or something? I'll wake you up."

"I don't want a nap." His eyes were bleak. "How about sex?"

There was something off. His mood was unreadable, and he'd never been so matter-of-fact about making love with her before. "Sex sounds good."

She thought she knew his every mood, but this was a new one. Nick didn't want to talk, didn't tease her or smile as he peeled her clothes from her body the moment they were inside the bedroom.

"Is everything okay?" she whispered the words, desperate to know how she could get the old Nick back. The old, carefree lover she'd begun to fall in love with.

"Fine." His gaze was shuttered—he was keeping something from her. Words wouldn't cut through the wall he'd erected, but maybe touch would.

She shoved her hands under his heavy sweater, and stroked his hard abs. Leaned back a little so he had room to strip it off his tee-shirt. Then her hands went to his belt.

He'd pleasured her so many times, but she'd never tasted him—he'd never let her.

"Summer." He grasped her upper arms, but she wouldn't be diverted.

"Let me. I want to." She undid his jeans, and shoved them down. The outline of his cock pushed against the soft cotton of his trunks, so with one hand she freed him, sliding from base to tip with a firm grip.

"Shit." He groaned.

Before he could reach for her again, she dropped to her knees and took him into her mouth. Her hands wrapped around the back of his thighs, a tremor went through her fingers. She licked, she sucked, she stroked him with her tongue, feeling the sweet sting of victory as his hands buried themselves in her hair, holding her close.

He couldn't hold back, and she didn't want him to. Her nipples peaked in the chill air of the bedroom, and wetness flooded her at the noises he made.

Her hands tightened around his thighs as she took him deeper than she ever would have thought possible.

"I can't..." He flexed.

Her head moved back and forth, faster, faster.

Until he couldn't hold back any more.

Afterwards, they curled up together in the big bed.

"You kill me, do you know that?" Nick's arm tightened around her. "I don't have any control where you're concerned."

His hand smoothed down her back, across the curve of her hip. "What's happened between us is crazy. Tomorrow is Christmas Eve, and in a couple of weeks you'll be gone. Back to your life. I'll miss you."

It felt as though a boulder was lodged in her throat, blocking words. "What if I didn't go? What if I stayed?"

"You can't." Nick's tone held a note of finality. "I know that, and you do too. You're an award-winning chef with a Michelin-starred restaurant. A woman with a glittering career. What could you do in Brookbridge, work in the coffee shop?" His laugh was harsh. "I'd love you to stay, but I couldn't ask you to give all of that up." His mouth brushed the top of her head. "We never planned any of this, and for good reason. There are a thousand reasons why we can't be together."

He pulled away and threw back the blanket that covered them. "We should get ready to go."

Tell him. Now. It was the perfect time. The only moment. And yet she stayed silent. Revealing that the restaurant was gone now, when she'd let so many opportunities pass her by, would be wrong. What they had couldn't even be called a relationship—and announcing out of the blue that there was nothing binding her to London any longer, she was free and planning to move back to Brookbridge in the near future, would come across as a demand to take their relationship to the next level.

She couldn't tell him like this.

She needed time before she made that sort of a commitment. She'd never wanted anyone as much as she wanted Nick, but...

"Are you getting out of that bed, or do I have to come in and drag you out?"

SIXTEEN

Ellie Logan was in her element. She fussed around everyone, welcoming Summer and Fella into the family with open arms—and dog treats. "He's gorgeous." She rubbed Fella's ears. "When Amy told me you'd adopted a dog I managed to get to the local shop to buy him something—if you'd let me know earlier, I'd have got a bone from the butcher's for him."

"He doesn't need a bone, Mum."

"He should have one. It's Christmas." She leaned down and spoke to the dog. "Shouldn't you, Fella? I'll get you one."

It was almost as if the dog understood—his tail wagged like crazy, and he panted with his mouth open.

"He's smiling." Ellie straightened, smiling herself. "He's lovely."

Summer had been dragged off by Nick's father to be introduced the other members of the family.

Ellie leaned close. "So, what's the story with you and Summer?" Her eyes were bright. "I like her a lot."

"You've only just met her." Nick glanced around, looking for a savior to rescue him from his mother's laser-like attention. A die-hard romantic, Ellie was always trying to set her children up with someone or other, and the pool of single Logans was a rapidly shrinking one.

"Well?"

He'd already told the story of how he'd met Fella—which of course included how he'd discovered Summer alone in her parents' house. "I couldn't leave Summer up there in the house alone without electricity."

"Of course not." Ellie patted him on the back, in very much the same way as she'd petted the dog. At least she didn't add "Good boy," although she was doubtless thinking it.

"And Declan asked me to look after her—to make sure that she didn't spend Christmas alone." He crossed his fingers at that one.

"Isn't she living with a man in London?"

It seemed nothing would deflect his mother's

determined digging for the truth. But which truth to tell? The story Summer'd spun to her family, which he'd believed false up until he'd seen Michael at the airport—or the story she'd told him, that they were over?

Split second decision. "That's over. I think Summer's re-evaluating her life at the moment."

"No better time to do it than at the end of the year." Ellie nodded. "She can start the new year fresh." She stood up straighter as the front door opened. "Ah, here's Finn and Val!" Leaving a waft of Chanel in her wake, his mother shot across the room in search of new blood.

Finn's wife, Val was a photographer, and she'd come armed. Her Nikon hung around her neck, and within moments, Ellie was organizing photographs.

Summer wandered over. "There's an awful lot of your family, aren't there?"

"Not really." Growing up the house had always been full to bursting. Friends of the Logan children were always welcome, and Ellie and Dermot's friends gravitated to the house where the kettle always seemed to be on the boil, and a fresh, warm, loaf of bread always ready to be sliced.

His parents were so gregarious they always had people over. Most of their nieces and nephews popped in regularly if they were in the area, and they had a wide circle of friends. But the best time of the year for both of them was Christmas, when every Logan was encouraged to come home from wherever in the world they'd settled.

"I guess I'm used to it." Nick looked down at Fella who sat at his feet. "I'm surprised he's not more freaked-out." He peered closer. His mother was right; the dog was definitely doing his best to smile.

"Right. You three." Ellie bore down, her hand curled around Val's arm.

"Hi, Val." Nick kissed her cheek. "This is Summer, and Fella. How are you?"

"Good." Val smiled back. "Busy."

"Now, squash in, with Fella between you." They obediently shuffled close.

"Arm around her." Ellie directed. "Say cheese."

They did as she asked while Val snapped away. Glanced at each other, smiling wide.

"That's great." Ellie looked around the room. "Dermot!" Grabbing Val's arm again, she set off across the room to her husband.

"I'll send you a link," Val called over her shoulder.

———

"VAL and I arranged the table like this deliberately," April Logan, wife of Matthew, confided. Across the table, the three Logan brothers sat shoulder to shoulder. "They should be appreciated in triplicate—don't you think?" Humor glinted in her eyes.

"Oh, definitely." Summer hadn't had so much fun for years. Both April and Val were so easygoing, it was easy to like them. And she was right—individually Nick, Matthew and Finn were devilishly good looking, but together...they were enough to give a woman a heart attack.

She didn't know Matthew, but Finn had been such a flirt he'd been impossible to forget. He was younger than her, younger than Nick, but he'd blazed through the female population of Brookbridge like a comet. Before he met Val at a speed-dating event and became a one-woman man.

"They are very good looking," she whispered to April.

"You're welcome." April passed over a bowl of mashed potatoes. "Just remember, if you're ever in charge of the table settings, this is the way we like to do it."

"Understood." She took the bowl, helped herself, and passed the bowl on to Val on her left.

"So, what do you do, Summer?" Val asked.

"I'm a chef."

"Thank God for that." Val passed the bowl of

potatoes down the table, and reached for a bowl of carrots. "You're here on Christmas Day?"

Summer nodded.

"I've never eaten anything Nick cooked—we've all been wondering how on earth he was going to manage producing anything edible—and I'm not much better. Matthew's the best cook of all of them."

"I'm sure he can't be that bad…" In her experience most people could cook if they had the right recipe, and followed it. "I'm not letting him off the hook by being here, I'll just supervise."

Val leaned close. "I think he lives on baked beans."

A memory of Declan and Nick seated at her mother's kitchen table with plates of beans on toast flashed in Summer's memory. Maybe Val was right…

"He did order a turkey. And it was the right weight." Across the table, she caught Nick's eye and smiled.

Everyone was eating, drinking, talking. The three Logan brothers were delivering a triple whammy of hot, but she only had eyes for Nick. *He's by far the hottest.*

"Did you say something?" Val leaned near.

"Jesus, did I say that out loud?" Summer's hand went to her heated cheeks.

"You did." Val grinned. "As long as you were talking about *your* Logan and not mine, you're safe."

My Logan. If she believed in Santa, she'd ask for her Logan for Christmas. "Well, I'm not sure he's mine, but I was talking about Nick."

Val surveyed Nick across the table with shrewd eyes. "Oh, I reckon he's yours alright. You've hooked him; you just need to reel him in." She reached for the bottle in the center of the table. "More wine?"

After dinner some members of the family drifted to the sofas next to the fireplace and began to play charades, while others stayed at the table, deep in conversation.

Summer's cell phone rang. She glanced at the screen surreptitiously under the table—*Michael. Again.* She bounced the call, and a moment later it rang again.

She rejected the call.

"I'll just let Fella out for some fresh air," she said to Val.

If she didn't call him back, he would doubtless ring again. And the last thing she wanted was to have a conversation with her ex while Nick was within earshot.

So she called him.

"Summer. Thank God. Where the hell are

you?" His voice was shrill—demanding. "I've been trying to track you down for days."

"I don't think my whereabouts are any of your concern, Michael."

"You're in Ireland." Satisfaction in his tone. "I know that much. I had to ring five of your friends to discover that you had gone home for Christmas. I flew out today and drove all the way up that bloody mountain to find the house empty."

What? Summer swiped her tongue over her dry lips. "What are you talking about?"

"I flew over to see you. I can't believe you didn't let me know the restaurant is up for sale. You should have told me."

He was unhinged. Delusional. "You and I are history; I didn't have to tell you anything. You made your feelings clear when you asked me to move out." Her hand was clenched tight, the tips of her nails digging into her palm. She opened her fingers wide and tried to calm down. "I don't want to see you. I suggest you go straight back to the airport."

"Where are you?"

"None of your business."

"Summer." He spoke her name, soft and pleading. A tone that once upon a time would have forced her to listen. *Not anymore.* "Please. I need to talk to you. I'm in the Brookbridge Hotel. Just an hour. Give me an hour of your time. You owe me that."

She owed him nothing, but curiosity spiraled through her. "I can't tonight." She blew out a breath. He was stubborn—there was no way he'd leave before he had seen her. She could rise early in the morning, get it over with..."I'll meet you tomorrow morning. One hour. No more."

"I'll be waiting." He hung up.

She shoved the cell phone into her pocket and went inside.

NICK HAD WATCHED from across the room as Summer checked her phone a couple of times. He knew who'd be calling. It had to be Michael.

She'd stood up, made some excuse, and headed into the kitchen.

He should just leave her alone—let her make the call in private, if that is what she intended. But instead, he excused himself from the group around the fire, and followed.

She was outside the back door, illuminated by the light that came on automatically anytime anyone went into the garden. Fella was sniffing around the perimeter. As Nick suspected, she was talking on the phone.

He couldn't make out the words, but she didn't look happy.

Frustrated, Nick strode to the wine rack and pulled out another couple of bottles of red.

The door opened. "Ah, there you are." He forced his voice to sound casual. "I was just getting..." He held up the bottles.

"I was letting Fella out." She avoided his eyes. Made no mention of the phone call. Then she walked to his side and linked her arm through his. "So, are we playing charades?"

"I guess." If she'd been talking to Michael, she should tell him—should be honest. But forcing her into a corner wasn't his style. Maybe she needed a little time—he could give her that. "We'll make our excuses in an hour or so—I don't know about you, but I've just about reached saturation point."

———

THE FOLLOWING MORNING, Summer parked outside the Brookbridge Hotel and then strode inside. Michael was sitting in the lobby, nursing a cup of coffee. The moment he saw her, he stood up and waved.

As if they were friends.

Every step toward him was like a step into the past.

He didn't fit here at all. His skin was lightly tanned from his regular sunbed sessions. His black, Hugo Boss suit fitted him to perfection, and he wore a dark pink paisley tie with his expensive white shirt. His shoes were so shiny; she bet if she peered closer she could see her face in them.

As she came closer, his hands came up as if to touch.

Hers came up too, palms first, in a don't-even-try-it gesture.

"Darling."

She arched a brow.

"Let's talk in my room."

She shook her head. "Here will be just fine." She sat on one of the leather tub chairs and placed her hands one over the other in her lap. "What is it, Michael?"

She was prepared for him to beg. For him to demand she came back to him and forgave him for throwing her out. But his next words shocked the hell out of her.

"You remember Marlon?"

Marlon White. Michael's wealthiest client. The man she'd wined and dined both at their home and at Summer's Kitchen. She liked Marlon, but they had never been friends.

"Of course."

"He told me Summer's Kitchen was for sale."

Michael's mouth tightened. "It was damned humiliating to have to admit I knew nothing about it." He glared at her as if he expected an apology.

"Tough."

He swallowed the last of his drink. "I don't know why you're being such a bitch, Summer." He ran his fingers through his perfectly coiffed hair. "Surely you realize..."

"You're a complete asshole. I don't need to listen to this." She picked up her bag from the floor.

His hand shot out and grabbed her arm. "Wait. Okay, I understand why you didn't tell me. We didn't end things well—maybe that was my fault. Anyway..." He gave her a smile, the smile that used to make her do whatever he wanted. "You don't need to worry about the future any longer. Marlon wants to buy Summer's Kitchen. And he wants you to continue on as head chef."

Simmering anger flashed to boil. "So you didn't come here for me...you came with a business proposition." How had she been so stupid not to realize that?

"Well, I have missed you." He looked hopeful. "Things had become difficult for us, you were so wrapped up in your work, in your financial difficulties—but with this new deal you won't need to worry about the money. Marlon will see to that side of the business and pay you a handsome salary. I think we could try again. I'd be willing to..."

"Forget it."

He frowned. "Okay, maybe that was too soon. But Marlon. You'll talk to him?"

"The realtor's details are on the sign." She stood. "Marlon is welcome to contact them and make a bid for the premises. But the name of the restaurant and its Michelin star is not for sale. Neither am I."

"Don't be stupid..."

She didn't even try to hide the contempt on her face. "Don't call me. If you can't explain to your richest client, give him my number and I'll talk him through it. I won't be returning to London, and there is no way I'll ever come back to you. Not for love or money." She looked at her watch. "Don't miss your plane."

SEVENTEEN

Brookbridge was full of shoppers. Nick was at his parents' house, and the thought of going back to his apartment held no appeal. Besides, Summer had presents to buy.

She headed to the small stores on Main Street, intent on finding at least a token for each member of the family who had so generously expanded their Christmas circle to include her. She picked up colorful scarves and gloves for April and Val, and a rather elegant fur trimmed hat for Ellie—and found a selection of tweed scarves in the local man's shop that she bought for the men. The presents were small, but she didn't know Nick's family well enough to choose anything more personal.

She bought a stocking full of dog treats for Fella.

For Nick? Nothing seemed right until she stood in front of the jeweler's window.

Moments later, she exited, clutching a small gold-colored bag. She fished her cell out of her bag, called Nick's cell, and asked to talk to Val.

"I wonder if you could forward those pictures you took of Nick, Fella and me to my cell phone?"

"Sure, no problem."

A few minutes later, they arrived in Summer's inbox. The chemist in Brookbridge had a sign in the window stating that they had a photo-printing machine, so she headed there next.

This time last year, she'd been busy in the restaurant—lunchtime of Christmas Eve had been one of their busiest days ever. She glanced over the road at the restaurant they'd eaten at the other night, *Buona Vita*. There was no way she'd get a table...not at such short notice, and without a reservation, but nostalgia for the atmosphere of a restaurant at Christmas made her walk across the road and push open the door.

She breathed in the scent of oregano, basil, roasted peppers.

"Hi." The blonde waitress, Elaine, recognized her. "You're Nick's friend." Her smile was welcoming. "Is it just a table for one?"

"I know you're busy..." There didn't seem to be an empty table in the place.

"We are. But I've just seated a sole customer at a table, and I did ask him if he'd be willing to share if we had someone else wanting to eat...would you mind sharing?"

Summer smiled. "I wouldn't mind at all."

"Great." Elaine led the way to a table near the window. A dark haired man in his early thirties was checking the menu. "Dr. Jones—may I seat this lady at your table?"

"Of course." The man gestured to the empty chair.

Elaine handed Summer a menu, and scurried away.

"John Jones." The man introduced himself.

"Summer Costello." She eased off her coat, and slung it over the back of the chair. "I really didn't think I'd get a table today."

"I didn't make a reservation either," John confessed. "I was working this morning, and just decided to call in on spec."

"You're a doctor, then."

"At the hospital. I came off the night shift, decided to do a bit of last minute shopping, and then thought I'd grab lunch before going home to sleep."

"I was shopping too." Summer scanned the

menu. "I had dinner here a few nights ago—their food is excellent."

There was silence for a few moments as they considered their choices, then John snapped his menu shut.

Elaine walked over immediately, her notepad at the ready.

"Would you like some water?" When she said yes, he picked up the jug from the middle of the table. "What do you do?"

"I'm a chef." She turned and gave Elaine her order.

To her relief, the doctor didn't feel the need to make any more small talk. Their meals arrived, and she attacked the lasagna, not realizing just how hungry she was. She'd ordered a glass of merlot, and sipped it between bites.

The restaurant was smaller than Summer's Kitchen—the menu choices simpler—but the food was expertly prepared, and the clientele were happy and appreciative. Every time a table was vacated, it was cleared and reset, and a constant stream of customers came through the front door, so many in fact, that they had a small crowd gathering, waiting for tables.

She was considering dessert when Elaine came over again, this time looking worried.

"I'm so sorry to disturb you." She clasped her

hands together as she spoke to John. "We have had an accident in the kitchen—the chef..." She swallowed. "I really don't want to ruin your meal, we've called for an ambulance, but..."

"Of course." John stood. He looked at Summer. "Excuse me."

He followed Elaine into the kitchen. The sound of a distant siren grew louder, and before long an ambulance turned the corner down the alley at the side of the restaurant.

Elaine returned, this time holding her notepad. "Can I take your dessert order?" Her eyes were bright and her smile forced.

"Is he all right?" Summer asked.

"The doctor thinks he may have had a heart attack." Elaine's bottom lip wobbled. "The chef is also the owner. He and his wife will be on their way to the hospital in the ambulance in a few moments."

The waitress looked shaken. "Sit down for a moment." It was the busiest time of day, on the busiest day of the year. The kitchen must be in uproar. Summer took a deep breath. "Listen, I'm a head chef. I don't know how everyone is coping back there in the kitchen, I'm sure the second chef has taken over, but if you need a hand back there, I'm more than happy to help."

Elaine's eyes widened. "But you don't know the menu..."

Summer could cook any one of the meals on the menu blindfolded. "Check with the second chef. See if he needs my help." She pushed her plate away. "You don't want to have to turn anyone away."

––––––

WHERE IS SHE?

Hours had passed since Summer's call—the call where she'd asked if Val was with him, and then asked to talk to her. She'd sounded relaxed and happy.

She'd made no mention of the mysterious phone call last night and they'd left his apartment at the same time that morning—him heading to his mother's house while she went into Brookbridge to do some last minute shopping. She'd dressed in a long black wool dress and high black boots for the occasion, had fastened her hair into a topknot and put on more jewelry and makeup than he'd seen on her this entire holiday. As if she was meeting someone.

He didn't want to be suspicious, but it was damn hard not to be.

Maybe there was a reason she hadn't replied to his text. Perhaps she was at home, waiting for him.

All the preparations that he could do today had

been done. Ellie was satisfied with progress. He'd caught up with his brothers, now it was time to find Summer.

He stuffed his arms into his coat and wrapped a scarf around his neck. "I'll be here early in the morning to deal with the turkey." He jerked open the front door.

April was staggering up the path laden down with packages. Nick held the door wide for her.

"You're leaving?" April's mouth turned down at the corners.

"Yes. Gotta go." He flattened himself against the wall so she could squeeze past him.

"Meeting up with Summer, then? I saw her in town having lunch in *Buona Vita* with some guy— I guess he's that brother I've heard so much about."

Nick couldn't get any words out—couldn't explain that Declan wasn't even in the country— instead; Nick forced a smile and got out of there as quickly as he could.

His heart sank on pulling up outside his dark apartment. He unlocked the door, turned on the lights and walked into the kitchen, Fella trotting along at his heels.

Everything was exactly as he'd left it—she hadn't been back.

He fed the dog, checked his cell phone again,

and walked upstairs. Her clothes still hung in the wardrobe—at least she hadn't moved out.

He called her. The phone must be on as it rang repeatedly but wasn't answered.

So what are you going to do about it? an inner voice demanded. The thought of Summer alone somewhere with Michael made him crazy. The bastard didn't deserve her. The prospect of losing her brought home the realization that he wasn't satisfied with a brief fling—she meant more to him than that.

They were more than a holiday romance, and he'd be damned if he'd let her just walk away, but right now, he was so angry she was ignoring his calls he couldn't see straight.

He could sit here, drown his sorrows in a bottle of Jameson, and wait for her to come back, or he could...

He sent her a text and then called Sean's number. "Hey, can I come over?"

"Sure. But don't you have a houseguest to entertain? Are you bringing her too?"

"I'm flying solo. Summer is out and I don't feel much like sitting here on my own."

"Great. Guys night. See you in a while, then."

Guys night. He and Sean had often hung out, downing whiskey, eating Doritos and watching action movies. They both dated up a storm, but neither was good at the commitment thing, so were usually alone on Christmas Eve. He'd thought this year would be different.

Nick called a taxi.

———

ONCE THE LUNCHTIME crush was over with, preparations for the dinner shift began. Summer had been enjoying herself so much, she'd become totally caught up in the moment. Cooking, without the pressure of being responsible for everything, was liberating. She'd forgotten just how much she enjoyed being a chef, working in a busy kitchen.

So when the second chef had come up empty trying to find another chef to cover at short notice for the evening booking, she hadn't been able to say no.

She checked her phone, but the battery was dead and she didn't know Nick's number, so without a charger she was stuck. Hopefully he'd understand.

The next few hours had flown. And she'd loved every minute.

When the last table had been served, she picked up her coat and bag, and made her excuses. Elaine called her a taxi, and a wad of notes was stuffed into her hand by the grateful owner, who had returned from the hospital to report that her husband, the head chef, was doing okay. They'd asked if there was any possibility she could help out more over the days to follow, but she'd declined.

Nick's apartment was dark when the taxi drew up.

She unlocked the front door, shrugged off her coat, and headed upstairs. His bedroom was empty. Confused, she grabbed the charger and plugged in her cell phone.

A couple of messages pinged into her in-box, she read the most recent first.

Have gone out. Call me when you get back.

Clear, concise, to the point. No x's at the end.

She glanced at her watch to see it was after midnight. Where is he? She called his number. "Nick? Hi, I'm home."

"And I'm out." His voice was slurred, as if he'd been drinking. "Good of you to call." He was a master of sarcasm; every word was dripping with it. "Did you enjoy yourself at the restaurant?"

Confusion swirled. How had he known where she was? "Yes, I just got carried away, I should have called, I'm sorry—"

"Forget it. It doesn't matter." The tone of his voice contradicted his words. "Listen, I'm at Sean's, and I've been drinking. I think I'll crash here for the night and go straight to my parents' house in the morning. If you come, bring the dog, will you?"

His attitude stunk. "Couldn't you grab a taxi?" She wanted to tell him about working in the restaurant, needed his arms around her. Waking up on Christmas morning with him as her present was an unrealized dream. "I'd really like to spend tonight with you." Her voice sounded husky, but she didn't care that her need was plain to hear.

"Sorry. I can't. Will you bring Fella tomorrow morning, or do I have to collect him?"

She bit down hard on her bottom lip. "I'll bring him."

"Goodnight, then."

Summer held the cell phone to her ear. He'd hung up on her.

After the call, Summer checked the earlier messages. A pleading one from Michael, begging her to reconsider. Two from Nick, asking her to call him.

The first was early afternoon, when she'd been busy in the restaurant kitchen—even if her battery was still working, she wouldn't have got it as Elaine had whisked her coat and bag away into the staff area for safekeeping.

How had Nick known she was at the restaurant? Her mind flickered back to the night of the Vet's Christmas Party—Nick's easy, friendly relationship with Elaine. Maybe she'd called him.

She rubbed the back of her neck. No. That made no sense. What possible reason could Elaine have for calling Nick and telling him that? She guessed she should have called him, it was Christmas Eve; she had no right to keep him hanging. But still, if he'd needed to talk to her so badly, couldn't he have rung the restaurant and asked to speak to her? He'd known she was there...

Summer was so tired she couldn't even think straight, so she changed into her nightgown and climbed into bed.

The sheets were cold. Outside the window, a gale was blowing, rattling the windows. If she'd called him, they'd be curled up here together.

All the way home, she'd imagined telling him about her day—sharing how exciting it had been to discover that her love of cooking hadn't been lost when she lost the restaurant. Now, cold reality pushed in. They never would have had that conversation. Because he had no idea what her life was really like—that nothing remained for her in London, or hadn't up until Michael's recent offer.

Up until that moment, she'd been mourning the death of a dream. Wallowing in self-pity for the misfortunes that life had dealt her.

When Michael offered her an escape—the

chance to continue running Summer's Kitchen, but without the pressure of ownership, everything sharpened into focus.

Summer's Kitchen was dead, and she had no desire to resurrect it. She didn't want to live in London any longer. Didn't want to try and recapture her old life. To deny, hide and fix her failures.

If she'd said yes to Michael's proposition, no-one would even have to know that she'd lost it all; that she'd so comprehensively failed. She could spin it any way she wanted—that she'd decided to sell the restaurant as a business decision, while retaining the cachet of being the chef whose name was over the door.

She could pretend.

Or she could tell the truth. Embrace the fact that she'd tried something, it hadn't worked out, and she had learned something important—how to fail.

There was a new life waiting, full of undreamed of possibilities. She had no time to waste on yesterday's life.

She pulled the blanket up around her ears and closed her eyes. Tomorrow would be a busy day; she'd need to hit the ground running.

EIGHTEEN

Nick had thought there could be nothing worse than getting up on Christmas morning with a hangover.

He was wrong.

Being hungover on Christmas morning with one hand stuck up a turkey's ass was way worse. A new admiration for his mother was born as he withdrew a small, slimy bag containing God knows what, and the turkey's severed neck from the body cavity and flung it into the trash.

"You should have saved that for the gravy," a voice said from the doorway.

Val. Clutching her ever-present camera, even though she was only dressed in pajamas.

"Want to stick your hand up there again and smile for me?"

Nick swallowed his initial response—Bugger off seemed an uncharitable Christmas retort—and shook his head. "No way. What are you doing up? It's barely eight." He frowned at her camera. "I thought you wouldn't have to work today."

"You're kidding, right?" Val pulled a couple of mugs from the cupboard, and spooned coffee granules into them. "Ellie has me on standby for the entire day. I'm supposed to record every single moment." She pushed her hair back from her face. "Especially all evidence of you cooking." While the water boiled, she wandered over and took a picture of the nude, raw, turkey, lying on a bed of foil in a baking tray. "Looks like I'm a bit early though."

She pointed the camera his direction, and snapped off a shot. "Can I ask about the sunglasses?"

Nick waved to the ceiling. "The kitchen light. My hangover..."

Val winced. "Hangover?" She grabbed another mug and readied it. "You need some coffee too then."

"Bring it on." He washed his hands.

Val made the coffee and brought a mug to the table. "I'm back to bed. See you later."

Was this how it always was? For years, Ellie

must have got up early doing all the preparations for Christmas lunch while her layabout family lazed in bed. "Aren't you going to help me?"

Val grinned. "I'll help with the vegetables in an hour or so, until then you're on your own." She glanced around. "Where's Summer? I thought she was on duty this morning with you."

"So did I." Nick drank a slug of coffee, then added another spoon of granules to the cup. Dark chestnut grounds swirled in miniature chunks on the surface, so he had to swirl up a mug whirlpool to disperse them.

"Looks like you have it covered." Clutching the two cups, and wearing a rueful smile, Val left.

Great.

His mother had presented him with the Christmas recipe book, which detailed a step by step of how to make everything, so he peered at the page for what was next.

Smear the outside of the bird with butter.

If and when Summer finally arrived, he felt damned tempted to smear *her* with butter. *Where the hell is she?*

Apparently, melting butter in the microwave was a fine art. One he hadn't mastered. The surface looked fine, but when he scooped up a handful, the inside was liquid, rather than soft. With a curse, Nick poured it over the top of the turkey and rubbed it in with his palm. If he'd written this bloody cookbook, he'd have done it differently. He would have written: "Take the butter out of the fridge the night before. Open the packet of bacon before you do the whole smearing butter thing, because the packet is impossible to open with slippery hands." Eventually it was done, with rashers of bacon overlapping on the bird's breast.

The book said: *stuff the neck end with the stuffing you've made*—so he squeezed in a couple of tubes of sausage meat.

Another hand wash, then he stuffed the whole thing into the oven with a sigh of relief.

"How's it going?" Ellie walked into the kitchen.

"I have the turkey in." He deserved a medal. Or at least a woo-hoo. He got a pat on the back.

"Why are you wearing sunglasses?"

He slipped them off and shoved them into the pocket of the apron. Which he looked ridiculous in —whoever thought it was a good idea to give his mother an apron with stripper legs in stockings printed on it was a damned idiot.

"I was hungover." The light didn't hurt any more, and the dull ache in his head had faded. "I think I'm over it now."

"Good. It's time for breakfast—the others will be down in a few minutes." She walked to the fridge and started to assemble ingredients. "I'm guessing you'd like me to do the fry?"

Every Christmas morning, Ellie provided a full Irish breakfast spread on the dining room table. While she was also preparing Christmas lunch. Who would have guessed her serene exterior covered a superwoman interior?

"How's your arm? They could just have toast."

Ellie's eyes widened. She planted her hands on her hips. "Nick Logan. My arm was just sprained, it's totally better now. You know perfectly well breakfast is part of the Christmas experience. You always loved it. What's different?"

"What's different is that I now know how much work this all is." He piled the dirty bowls into the sink, turned on the faucet, and squirted detergent under the stream of hot water. "I've barely started—there's so much to do. How on earth do you manage to make breakfast as well?"

"I'll cook breakfast." She took a bottle of champagne from the fridge, and a carton of orange juice. "You make the drinks. I've found that the orange juice helps. It must be the vitamin C."

The booze, more like.

He put glasses out on a tray. Poured in a measure of orange juice into each one, and topped them up with champagne, while Ellie grilled sausages and rashers, whipped up scrambled eggs, and made toast.

"Pass me over a glass, and have one yourself," Ellie said. "Cooks' privilege."

Footsteps on the stairs. Then one by one, the rest of the family poured into the room and descended on the mimosas, like a murder of crows landing in the top branches of a beech tree.

———

THE DOORBELL WORKED; it pealed inside the house, but five minutes later, Summer still stood on the doorstep, clutching Fella's lead.

She pressed the bell again, hopping from foot to foot in an attempt to keep warm.

A shadowy outline appeared in the frosted glass panel in the front door, grew larger, and then the door was opened. Nick's father stepped back to let her enter. "We were wondering where you'd got to." Dermot bent and rubbed Fella's ears. "Come on in, everyone is at breakfast."

She couldn't believe she'd slept in—today of all days. Her insomnia had struck again last night. Her body had been tired after the double shift in the restaurant, but her mind had been racing like a greyhound on a dog track. She'd said no to a job at the restaurant, but hadn't made it a definite refusal, stating instead that she didn't know exactly what the new year would bring.

She'd wanted to talk to Nick about it. She still wanted to talk to Nick, needed to understand if his attitude the previous night had been born from irritation that she'd not contacted him, or a different reason. If there would be a chance for them he'd have to accept that her profession had unattractive working hours. By the early hours, she'd at least worked out a few things. That she wanted to move back to Ireland. To Brookbridge. And she wanted Nick to be part of her future.

She wouldn't hide the facts any longer, surely he would understand why she'd hidden the truth of the restaurant from everyone?

She shed her coat, wooly hat, and gloves in the hall, and followed Dermot into the dining room.

Conversation at the table silenced for a moment as everyone looked at her, then Ellie stood up and waved at the sole, unoccupied seat. "Come and have some breakfast, love."

Nick's face was impossible to read. He called Fella over and showered all his attention at the grateful dog. She sat down next to him, a chill seeping into her bones as he refused to look her direction.

"Good morning." She addressed her comment directly to him—knowing the presence of others would mean he'd have to reply. "I'm sorry I was late, I overslept."

"Good morning." His gaze flickered to her, but he didn't smile. "I'll just give Fella his bone." He stood and walked into the kitchen.

Ellie set a plate in front of her, and Val passed a dish of sausages.

She had to talk to him. "Excuse me for a moment." She stood up and dashed into the kitchen after Nick.

She walked to him, and touched his arm. "Why are you being so distant?"

He pulled back. "I'm not distant." His mouth compressed. "What do you want from me, Summer? Congratulations?"

She frowned.

"Look. I understand. You and I were only ever going to be a short-term thing—you wouldn't even consider letting your brother know about us. I would have liked to have more time with you, but it didn't work out. Don't make a big deal about it."

There was a pain in her chest. "Are you ending things with me?" Happy bloody Christmas.

The sound he made was closer to a bark than a laugh. "Don't push this all on me. You're the one..."

"Summer, your breakfast is getting cold," Ellie said from the doorway. "Come back in. We're opening the presents in a minute."

Never had a group of people been more annoying, even when they were trying not to be. Val kept snapping photographs, and when breakfast was over, the presents were dragged from beneath the tree and distributed. "I've left mine in the hall." She dashed out to retrieve the large bag she'd stowed with her coat.

She had to give Nick that present. The one she'd thought perfect just the day before, but which now seemed horribly inappropriate.

"Here's one for you, Summer." Val handed over a beautifully wrapped parcel.

"And one from me." April shoved a present wrapped with penguin-covered paper her direction. "Is everything okay with you and Nick?" She glanced over. "Did you have a fight?"

"I haven't seen him since yesterday morning, he was out last night." And he didn't come home, even when he knew she was there, waiting. "He's angry with me over something."

"Is your brother back in town?"

What? "My brother lives in Spain. My parents are out there right now for Christmas. What made you think he was here?"

"Ah." April rubbed the back of her neck. "I saw you yesterday, with a man. I thought he was your brother—I told Nick..."

Understanding flooded her, as if someone had

turned on a light in her head, banishing the fog of confusion. "Nick knows I was with a man yesterday?"

Before either of the women could respond, Elle was there, shoving a parcel into Summer's hands.

It was impossible to talk in the crowd of Logan's clustering around the tree, but at least she had some idea of why Nick was acting so strangely. He knew about her meeting with Michael. She reached into the bag and pulled out her stack of wrapped parcels and started to distribute them.

When she was done, only one more remained to be given. Clutching it, she walked to Nick.

———

SHE'S HERE. When Summer hadn't turned up that morning, he'd thought he must have totally screwed up last night. Last night, he'd drowned his sorrows in a bottle of whiskey, and had snapped out a few terse words to her when she'd eventually called, instead of doing what he yearned to—to lay his feelings out there, to ask her to choose him, rather than Michael. But she was here. And she was trying to connect.

Even now, when he'd given her no opening.

Nick blew out a breath and picked up the small

wrapped box he'd shoved under the tree. When he straightened, she was in front of him.

"This is for you." She held out a small, gold bag. "It's not much, but I thought it was perfect."

I thought it was perfect too, I thought we were perfect. "Thank you." For the first time that day, he smiled at her. "And this is for you. I hope you like it." They exchanged gifts. "I'm sorry I was being a bit of a jerk earlier."

Her lips turned up at the corners in a half-smile. "I guess I gave you cause. My cell phone died last night, I would have called if I could."

Everything about her, the way she leaned in a little to him, the glance that flickered from his eyes to his mouth, her smile, showed she wasn't indifferent. She was here, when she could still be in a hotel room with Michael. He didn't know what that meant, but it was an opportunity he wasn't prepared to squander.

"Thank you." He leaned in. So close he could see her pupils expanding. He wanted to kiss her more than he wanted anything, but if he started, he'd never stop.

Her lips softened and her hands rested on his chest. He breathed in the scent of flowers that hung around her in a fragrant mist. When he pulled back, her breathing had quickened. There were too many damned people around. "Come into the kitchen with me." He placed the bag she'd given him down on a nearby table. "Now."

Her eyes widened. She put the small box onto the table. Nick curled his fingers around hers and walked her out of the room.

In the kitchen, he closed the door and backed her against it. "Tell me you want me." His hands were at her waist, his face inches from her own. He wasn't playing any longer, was done with playing it cool, waiting. She's here. That had to mean something.

He kissed her mouth, trailed his lips down the curve of her jaw, then down her neck. She was wearing a dress with a deep V in the front, the curves of her breasts driving him wild. He cupped one breast, and she arched her neck and groaned.

"Your family is just next door..."

"I don't care." He bent his knees so they were at the same level, claimed her mouth again. Being without her wasn't an option. She had something to go back to in London, but he'd make it as difficult as he could for her to walk away—he'd show her how much she had come to mean to him.

When Summer's arms came up and wound around his neck, his heart jumped.

When she stepped her legs apart, and pressed herself as close as she could get, his body responded instantly.

When someone twisted the doorknob, he jerked his mouth away from hers, and growled, "Go away."

Whoever was on the other side did what they were told.

"Nick. We can't. Not here." She was breathing heavily and her eyes were drugged with lust.

"Tell me you want me."

Her tongue swiped over her bottom lip. "I want you."

"How much?"

"More than anything."

He rested his forehead against hers and let his hands fall. "I don't care that you've kept secrets from me. You're here, now, that's all that matters."

She tried to speak, but he placed a finger on her soft lips.

"We want each other. We choose each other. Everything else is unimportant."

He eased back, and took a step away. "Tonight, you'll sleep in my bed."

"And we'll talk." There was determination in her voice, in the unwavering way she looked at him. "I have things I need to tell you. Things to explain."

About Michael. He didn't think he could take it if she told him she'd slept with her ex again, but he'd have to try. Because whatever had happened the previous night, she'd chosen to be here today, with him.

"Tonight." He nodded. "We'll talk tonight."

———

THE NEXT FEW hours passed in a haze. They were never alone. The kitchen was a buzz of activity. Val, April and Ellie joined them in the kitchen, preparing vegetables and stirring sauces, while the men set the table and cleared up.

They weren't alone, but a silent thread tied them together evident in the looks they shared, the casual touch of a hand when passing ingredients one to the other, the way Nick brushed against her in passing. Deliberately. Laden with intent.

Later, they'd be alone. The scale of what she'd hid from him was large. What she'd hid from everyone. Would they think less of her when they discovered she'd failed?

She'd reveal the truth to Nick tonight, at home, and let the news percolate through his family gradually. She always spoke to her parents in the early evening on Christmas Day so she'd tell them the truth too.

When the meal was made, everyone carried dishes to the table that had been dressed in a beautiful white linen tablecloth and set with gleaming silverware. Ellie had lit candles in the center of the table, and the entire scene was magical.

Nick carried in the turkey and placed it in front of his father.

"I'm proud of you, son." Dermot picked up a lethal looking knife and started to carve. "This looks fantastic."

"Remind me to make a bet with you again next year," Ellie added. "I like not being responsible for Christmas dinner."

Finn walked around the table filling everyone's glasses with champagne.

Someone's cell phone rang. Nick reached into his pocket and glanced at the screen. "It's Declan." His steady gaze met Summer's.

They expected her to be in the house with Michael. The moment she'd hoped to put off was here. Now. She moved her head in a tiny movement —a brief nod.

"Put him on speakerphone," Ellie said.

"Yes, do. We'd all like to wish him merry Christmas," Dermot added.

Nick answered the phone. "Hey, Declan. Merry Christmas. We're all at the table and you're on speakerphone."

"Happy Christmas to you all." Her brother sounded happy. "If you're all sitting down to lunch, I won't keep you. Did he do a good job, Ellie?"

"Well it looks and smells brilliant. I think I'll have to get Nick to cook every year," Ellie said.

"So, who is around your Christmas table this year? Full house?"

"Hi, Declan, this is Finn, I'm here with Val. Happy Christmas from us."

One by one, the family introduced themselves and wished her brother the best of the season. Then it was her turn.

"Happy Christmas, Declan." Her voice was so quiet she sort of hoped he hadn't heard. *No such luck.*

"Summer? What are you doing there? I thought you and Michael..."

"The Logans kindly asked me to join them." Everyone was looking at her. She swallowed and curled her hands into fists on her lap. "Michael isn't with me." Her face heated. God, this whole situation was beyond embarrassing. "Michael and I are over. We've been over for months—I didn't want to tell you, I knew you'd all want me to join you in Spain rather than be alone for Christmas." It was the truth, but not the entire truth. Summer picked up her glass and drank deeply. "The truth is, I didn't want to admit that I'd failed."

"Finishing with Michael isn't failing, it's a win. I for one am delighted—the guy was a prick...uh... Sorry for the language, Ellie."

Summer's pulse was racing. Her heart was hammering so hard it hurt. Nick reached out and placed his hand over hers.

"What about the restaurant, Summer? A friend told me he walked past it a couple of days ago...he said—"

Summer's stomach dived. She didn't want it to come out like this, she wanted to tell Nick the truth first, but there was no way to now, no way out.

"I lied about everything. It's not just Michael— I've failed at the restaurant too. Summer's Kitchen has closed and the premises is on the market." Shocked faces and gasps met her announcement. "Can you take me off speakerphone, Nick? I think I need to talk to Declan for a moment in private."

Nick turned speakerphone off and handed his cell phone over.

"Start without me," Summer said to the table in general, then she took the phone and retreated into the kitchen.

Adrenaline coursed through her veins as Summer sank onto a chair. Her brother was talking non-stop, but all she could think of was the faces that had stared at her. One face in particular. Nick's face. He'd looked stunned by her revelations. And right now, he was doubtless facing the forth degree from his entire family.

"You should have told us," Declan said.

"I didn't want to disappoint everyone." Her chest felt tight. "I've always been—"

"What? A winner? You've always excelled at everything. That's just who you are, Summer. But it isn't the reason your family loves you. We love you because you're you. Jeez, as your younger brother, I love you despite the fact that you're so perfect."

"What do you mean?" Her forehead pleated.

"You were a prefect. Head girl. A straight A student. Everything competition you entered, you won. It would have been easy to resent you—and I won't lie, when I was younger I used to get so frustrated. I struggled with stuff that came so easily to you."

Declan had never given her even a hint of his feelings. Or had he? Had she been so wrapped up in her own life she'd not even noticed? "I don't know what to say."

"You don't have to say anything. You just have to realize that not being perfect was not an issue for Mum and Dad. They love us both the same. Failing at something is normal. Going through it alone isn't. We're here for you. My admiration for you isn't dented one bit by knowing Summer's Kitchen has closed. I love you. I hate the fact you've had to go through all of this—and the end of your relationship —without anyone." He was silent for a moment. Then, "Does Nick know all this?"

"He does now."

Declan puffed out a breath. "Christ, did you just tell everyone for the first time?"

"Yes. Nick knew I wasn't with Michael, but—"

"Back up." Declan's tone was sharp. "Nick knew you and Michael were through and he didn't tell me?"

"I asked him not to. Nick's been great. He's helped me so much over the past few days, I...I have feelings for him."

"What?" Declan swore. "What the hell do you mean, you have feelings for Nick? He's supposed to be...Damn, I told him to take care of you. I didn't mean for him to—"

Anger flared. "I care about Nick. I care about him a lot. I don't need you to tell me who I can date..."

"You're vulnerable," Declan said flatly. "You don't know what you're doing. I never would have thought Nick would take advantage of you. I know he's been crazy about you forever..."

He has?

"But he has no damn right in hitting on you when you're just out of a relationship. No damn right."

"My relationship with Nick is none of your business, Declan. I know he's your best friend, and I know you're protective of me, but I didn't walk into this blind, and I'm not on the rebound." She breathed in deep. "I'm in love with Nick."

"So when were you both going to tell me this?"

"Well, I guess I wanted to tell Nick first. I'd planned to tell him tonight."

"Mum and Dad want to know what's going on."

She couldn't go through it all again. "Everyone here is eating. I have to go back to the table and explain." It was a big ask, but she had to delegate. "Could you tell Mum and Dad? I'll call later."

NINETEEN

Summer looked subdued when she came back. She crept across the room and sat down, a nervous smile on her face.

"I'm sorry about all that," she said to the table in general. "I didn't mean to unload all of my personal baggage at the table."

"So the restaurant is closed?" Nick asked.

"Yes. It has been for a while. There's so much competition in the restaurant business, especially in central London—I tried, but..." Her shoulders rose and fell in an eloquent shrug.

"And your relationship broke up as a result?" Ellie leaned forward. The curiosity in her eyes was mixed with concern. "I'm so sorry to hear that, dear."

"Michael and I broke up before Summer's Kitchen closed. I moved out months ago. He wasn't happy that I was talking about the problems with the restaurant so much. I guess he just wanted everything to be perfect. To stay perfect."

"But he came to see you yesterday." Nick crossed his arms. This conversation should be taking place in private—the last thing he wanted was for his entire family to see how much he cared about Summer, but somehow he couldn't stop talking. "Are you going back to him?"

With a gasp, she reached out to grasp his arm. "No. Never. He called and wanted to meet. I really had no inclination to listen to anything he had to say, but I knew he wouldn't leave without seeing me. I went to his hotel yesterday." She stared into Nick's eyes. "I'm sorry I didn't tell you. I should have. I thought he was going to beg me for a second chance, and I was ready to tell him that would never happen. That I cared for someone else."

Nick wished that his family would talk amongst themselves rather than watch Summer with such intense focus, but it was as if everything playing out in front of them was too interesting to turn away from.

"He didn't want me he wanted the business. Michael had a client who wanted to buy the restaurant and employ me as head chef. I guess he was keen to buy the whole package, Michelin star and all. I have absolutely no interest in doing that— Summer's Kitchen is dead, as is my life in London. I plan to move back to Brookbridge in January." Her hand stroked down Nick's arm until it found his hand.

Nick gripped her hand tight.

"I was only with him for an hour, then I went shopping."

She's lying. The only reason he could think of was that she didn't want to admit that she'd spent the evening with Michael. She must have slept with him. Bitter bile rose in Nick's throat. He pulled his hand from hers. "I care about you, Summer, but I can't be with someone who lies to me."

"Holy God, has there been romance going on between you two?" Ellie breathed. Dermot shushed her.

"You were seen with him later in the restaurant —you didn't deny it when I mentioned it this morning, and you didn't come home last night until past midnight. Whatever is between you and Michael doesn't seem to be over." He couldn't sit at the table any longer listening to her lies. Nick stood.

Summer jumped to her feet. "Don't you run away from me, Nick Logan. Yes, I was in the restaurant—I decided I wanted to have lunch there alone but Elaine seated me at a table with a stranger. The head chef had a heart attack and was taken away in an ambulance. They needed me to step in and help, so I did. I cooked the rest of the lunches, and then started prepping the evening menu. I should have called you—but my phone was dead, and then I got caught up in all that had to be done. If you don't believe me, phone Elaine, she'll tell you."

The fervent light in her eyes proved she was telling the truth. "So you spent yesterday cooking? I thought..."

"You thought I was with Michael?" Her eyes softened. "You thought I spent last night with Michael and yet you were still willing to hear me out—still wanted to be with me?"

"Yes." Nick slipped an arm around her waist and pulled her close. "I thought you were with him, but the fact that you came home last night, the fact that you came here today, was more important than anything that had gone before. You'd made your choice. You chose me."

Summer touched the side of his face. "I do choose you. I want you not just for Christmas but for always."

He had to kiss her. It didn't matter that his entire family was sitting around their Christmas table, mouths agape. It didn't matter that he'd opened his heart and spilled his guts in full view of his brothers who would doubtless tease him about this moment for the rest of his life. "I love you." He pressed his mouth against hers, to the sound of applause, laughter and catcalls.

———

AT LONG LAST, they sat alone before the fire in the sitting room, Summer on Nick's knee, while the rest of the family washed up in the kitchen.

"We never opened our gifts to each other." She reached around him to the small table and grabbed them. "Here." Now everything was out in the open, the freedom to kiss him was irresistible, so she brushed her lips against his. "Merry Christmas."

Nick reached into the gold bag, pulled out a box and opened it. Nestling in a bed of sky blue tissue lay a crystal snow globe, with a gold loop at the top for attaching to a tree. He shot her a confused look. "A Christmas decoration?"

"Take it out."

Nick picked it up and turned it around in his hands. The snow globe was cleverly constructed to hold a photograph. She'd cut around the picture of Nick, Summer and Fella that Val had taken and mounted it inside. Tiny, polystyrene beads formed snowy ground at their feet. Nick shook it. "It's beautiful."

A tiny tableau to record how they'd met, how all three of their lives had become intertwined forever.

Nick placed the crystal ornament back into its box. "Now you open yours."

The box he'd given her was wrapped in dark green paper and tied with gold ribbon. She opened it. Inside, was a thin gold chain. A gold Claddagh pendant hung from it. Two hands holding a golden heart.

"I wanted to show you that you hold my heart in your hands." Nick brushed her hair away from her face. "I think you always have." He picked up the necklace and fastened it around her neck.

"I haven't told you yet—but I love you." The door nudged open. Fella trotted in and curled around their feet in the fire's warmth. Summer snuggled close and whispered in Nick's ear. "Do you think we can go home soon?"

———

IT SNOWED CHRISTMAS NIGHT. And for three long days after. Nick and Summer were snowbound in his apartment, and she couldn't think of anything more perfect. But every magical interlude had to end sometime—and on the fourth day Summer woke to the sound of Nick on the phone.

"That was Sean." He walked across the bedroom to her, gloriously naked. They'd made love for days on end, and still the sight of him had her reaching for him. "I have to go out."

She sat up in bed.

"Ah, don't tempt me." His gaze travelled over her exposed body. "I want to crawl back into bed and make love with you again, but there's a flock of sheep buried on a farm outside town. They're digging them out now—some are dead already and the others suffering from hypothermia. I need to help Sean." He started to pull on his clothes.

"Can I help?" She climbed out of bed and picked her clothes off the chair.

"No, we can manage."

The doorbell rang. Fella barked. "Is he coming to pick you up?" Summer wriggled into her skinny jeans, pulled on a tee-shirt and topped it with an Aran sweater.

"No, he's already at the farm." Nick sat down on the bed to put on his socks and shoes.

"I'll get it." Summer shoved her feet into her slippers and padded downstairs. "It's all right, Fella." She opened the door to the sitting room and ushered the dog in. The doorbell rang again. "I'm coming!"

She pulled the door open, then stood there,

surprise striking her dumb. Her mother, father, and brother on the doorstep. "What—"

Before she could get another word out, she was clasped into her mother's arms, the recipient of a hug that would break ribs. "We couldn't wait any longer, we had to come and see you." Her mother's face lit up with her smile.

"Let us in, will you, Sis?"

Summer stood back to let her family enter.

Fella let out an impressive howl. She opened the door to the sitting room to put him out. "It's all right, Fella, these are friends." He sniffed the visitors, tail wagging. "This is the dog we rescued," she said.

Declan stepped close. "I'm concerned about you. You're just out of one relationship, you shouldn't be diving straight into another."

"It's not like that. Michael ended it with me four months ago, but our relationship had been failing for a long time before then. I just didn't want to acknowledge it." What had once seemed so impossible to explain now came easy. Her relationship had failed because Michael was the wrong person for her—she'd never really loved him, not the way she loved Nick. "I was unhappy for a long time, but not any longer."

She looked up at a noise from the stairs. *Nick.*

Declan walked to his friend, spine straight, jaw tight. "You and my sister, huh?"

"You're my best friend in the world." Nick stared Declan in the eye. "And Summer is the woman I love. I hope you'll be happy for us."

Declan's head tilted to the side, considering.

"I wish I could stay and talk, but I have to get to a medical emergency." Nick picked up his sheepskin coat and shoved his arms into it. "I'm glad you're here though." His gaze was unwavering. "Because I have a question I planned to ask you in the New Year. I want your blessing, Declan. I want you to be okay with me proposing to Summer."

"You want to..." Summer couldn't get the words out.

"You have it." Declan smiled and thumped his friend on the back.

Nick looked at Summer's father, who nodded.

"You haven't even..." Would all their most significant moments be played out in front of an audience?

"Summer." Nick clasped her hands. "This isn't the way I wanted to do it. I don't even have a ring yet." He brought her hands to his mouth and kissed her fingers. "I wanted to talk to Declan privately and then ask you..."

He was on his way out of the door—animals

stranded in the cold needed him. "You have to go."
She started to button his coat.

"Will you? Will you marry me?"

No ring, no romantic dinner, no suitor on his
knees, but a perfect proposal nevertheless.

She knew what she wanted; she wanted this
man, forever. "I will." She fastened the last button.
"Take care out there." She went up on tiptoe to kiss
him. "And hurry back."

AFTERWORD

I hope you enjoyed Snowbound Summer. All of the Logan series are available in large print, as is my Under the Hood series, and I am making large print editions of the rest of my backlist too!

If you'd like to get an email when my next book is released, you can sign up to my newsletter here: http://eepurl.com/r1m5H Your email address will never be shared and you can unsubscribe at any time.

Word-of-mouth is crucial for any author to succeed. If you enjoyed the book, please consider leaving a review at Amazon, even if it's only a line or two; it would make all the difference and would be very much appreciated!

Printed in Great Britain
by Amazon

34527688R00139